Dust, Spittle and Wind

Sanya Osha

Langaa Research & Publishing CIG
Mankon, Bamenda

Publisher:
Langaa RPCIG
Langaa *Research & Publishing Common Initiative Group*
P.O. Box 902 Mankon
Bamenda
North West Region
Cameroon
Langaagrp@gmail.com
www.langaa-rpcig.net

Distributed outside N. America by African Books Collective
orders@africanbookscollective.com
www.africanbookcollective.com

Distributed in N. America by Michigan State University Press
msupress@msu.edu
www.msupress.msu.edu

ISBN:9956-579-28-9

DEDICATION

For George Herault

Now your suffering really continues … oh truly continues after promises of redemption and freedom. A freedom that is supposed to combine the trappings of supreme idleness and everlasting bliss. The importance of work is underscored by fantasias of indolence and utopia after the banality of dystopia. But on the contrary the condition of your existence is marked by the beginnings of another protracted period of struggle. Struggle, struggle, struggle after the Hitlerian fashion (without of course the same steeliness of breath, heart and loins) and which immediately conjures *Mein Kampf* with its diabolical turgidity, sordidness, heinous rigidities and all that fuss. The last thing one expected after the termination of the previous dynamic of struggle was the commencement of another season of rigour and subjection. Instead every sinew of one's being craved expanses of remuneration and divine repose. Not so, you had to accept the irritants of a fourth-rate discipline together with its ideological masks. What lie behind the masks one may ask? Pestilential vices that are incapable of developing their own strategic objectives or principles of furthering the aims of their own wrath. A diseased ocean rises at the end of the sunset continent and flashes before your eye, there you see it losing the power of its own evil argument. It's all part of the same thing, the same network and the same bad economy. The arguments aren't simply pursued to their logical conclusions. One isn't able to quantify, to analyse because the whole architecture is devoid of the most basic skills.

It all started when some khaki politicians started bellyaching about patriotism, no, to be more precise, nationalism. About the youngest and best grade of blood running amok to cleanse the sleaze and rot of the land, no, the nation to be exact. One was meant to go the dreariest municipalities and the most wretched hovels in the name of national service. Very commendable one may add. It is always humane to offer some life-uplifting service to one's fellowmen. Many would contend that it is a keystone of progress. Yeah no sweat since it is so easy to blab over the warm graves of the meek and weak. One really needs to find out whether the ever so fine qualities of this argument can be logically concluded, empowered and then enacted.

When you are called, it was something akin to conscription, you just get up and go. Go, go, go, says the oppressor khaki man and so you go. And like the rest he went to the farthest point in the north where the sun was daily smothered in its own heat. There was no blues here, just slow red, deadly funk, it stung you between the eyes and made you hiss between your teeth the word heat. Olu Ray is his name. He is as characterless as a wisp of air, a mere sampler of uneven experience looking for the kind of strength that would reconstitute him. One could observe if one was perceptive enough that the fibre of his being was air drifting through all the poles of the earth and leaving no traces. He was on a desperate search for liver power. But this form of tracelessness was not peculiar to him alone. The nation he was to serve had many traceless characteristics. Files go missing and statistical accountancy was anathema. One got to make phenomenal formlessness a way of life. No one really complained, after all what was there to complain about since the majority had adopted this particular manner of existence as its credo. This is not to say that Olu Ray personified the spirit of his nation. Far from it. He was simply too metaphysical to connect with the most elemental points of conflagration in the land of his birth. He was overwhelmed by a dreamy, far-off idealism that dulled his senses at the most vital levels. He just gladly let things slide by. But the northern border city to which he had been posted was the antithesis of his temperament in the sense that the heat gave off an inexorable brightness. Bright red heat that had no funk, no dark serpentine fumes, no warm, moist heat of the loins, no lush green meadows slowing sinking into steady, intense pre-Raphaelite dissipation, no sickening corruption of

2

ancient romance, no lyrics of beatitude from the green preservation commune. Oh fire was always close by and one couldn't simply ignore its political connotations. Your friend with whom you ate from the same dish could turn out to be you slayer when swords come flying borne by the horses of the harmattan. Wild desert gales accompanied by slow desert sands. At such times you really wished you had prepared yourselves for such cataclysmic days of reckoning. You really wished you had listened to the low grumblings of fear in your expectant blood. But one would have sometimes heard the bored misanthrope groan-I want to go back home. Yet he knows within the depths of his sorrowing that home is really a small place to be in.

*****

Olu Ray had not wanted to go to the border of the city to which he had been posted. Before he finally decided to go, he had passed through the throes of a most crushing dilemma. To go or not to go? In the process of this internal toing and froing, his physical equilibrium gave way and he would babble to complete strangers showing his fears in the harshest lights. To venture forth or to disengage? The shades of information he received tugged him in various directions until he momentarily lost his presence of mind. Inordinate multivalency leads to an acute loss of focus. In its place a hazy brightness reeled slowly as if narcoticised. Nonetheless he was able to perceive his pain sharply. No one needed to inform him that he was bleeding. Soon people started to snap at him; "get up and go", "don't be a slob". One afternoon when no one was expecting it, he left without saying goodbye. He promised himself that he would not write to anyone either. On his first dawn in the border city, he was greeted by a great deluge of flies. They kissed every inch of his face until he grew tired of waving them away. They seemed like his most devoted fans and he wasn't so keen on losing his only constituency. And then the sun rose from behind its dusky blue throne like a scarlet celestial serpent. It seemed to pursue you relentlessly to the ends of the shades. Your body could no longer retain water, it kept losing it. Soon, other matters apart from the elements began to engage his senses. The people around him who went about like automatons. Overnight zombies, one might call them. He found them quite amusing and baffling as they were supposed to be drawn from the nation's brightest fount of blood. But to him they seemed like the residue of coarse steel. He tried looking into their eyes hoping to break the regime of hypnosis but their eyes looked through him to heed the puppet masters. It was a farce quite alright but there was no one he could enjoy it with. In the end, his isolated resistance was broken and he eventually fell in with the throng who were being trained in the ways of mindless servitude. Clichés have many techniques of winning the day. Day by day he lived as if in a dream. But it didn't matter. Most lived as if in a dream.

The day began for all at five thirty when the man with the bugle fractured their lazy, inchoate dreams at dawn. Moments later they scrambled into their khaki uniforms and ran to the parade ground for the morning roll-call. And then military drill began. Left right , left right- right about turn. Stand as you are! Close drill. One, two, three bounce the leg into the dust until it breaks after all it is a leg that has been bought by the government. One two top three. A military cant that seems to have evolved out of a poorly hatched civil war. The English is not very good. No perhaps it is more accurate to say the English has since lost its colonial purity. It has become an adulteration of distant Portuguese sounds, hundreds of local dialects that would eventually become extinct, the gaggling of delta swamps, poor lessons from half-formed educational institutions and the mad cries of civil war.

But no, no, no. We shall have to describe where the servants of the nation are domiciled. Not hard to do. The road to the site stretches out away from the town centre. It unfurls to pass expanses of open savannah country dotted by stunted *dongoyaro* trees planted to check the ravages of desertification. During sand storms dust particles are whipped up and flung far and wide. The effect can be very unpleasant on the eyes. Not only the eyes suffer; clothes become dirtied as one sometimes has to fling oneself to the ground to avoid the force of dust-ridden winds. Desert guitar blues do serenade us about the beatitudes of the endless universe of sands. Grant us the patience to see the unfolding light and shade of its faces, the dances of its veiled maidens and rumoured sweetness of its milk. Desert guitar blues grant us the fortitude to ignore the sourness of its cheeses. On the way to the site, one sees settlements too small to be called hamlets. Four or maybe five hovels struggling above the land in utter isolation. Anyone there? No, a goat crosses the ghost land like an epiphanic ghost wind chewing obviously, the curd of bitterness. Pass on we shan't die just yet.

A desolate sign-post announces our destination. The drive then resumes another dimension. More stunted trees floundering underneath the subversive vastness of the sun. There are a few tomato stalls with produce that seem larger than life. This is some consolation when one considers the harshness of plant and shrub texture. Very unwelcoming to say the least.

Close to the site is however a real hamlet of say ten to fifteen huts. The inhabitants are hardly noticeable. But one gets the impression that there is humankind present and flourishing on a very low key level. The site has many large playgrounds and open spaces for games and other out-door events. The servants are harboured on a ratio of five to six in a dusty room. Dusty is the word since one must always remember that this is indeed dust country. The cobwebs are something to blab about. Otherworldly to put it more graphically. For those who suffer from asthma and severe gastric catarrh the ordeal is nightmarish. The more one sweeps, the more the dust returns in folds and dunes. After all this is the country of dust. The little dust-covered girls who wear thick stale make-up selling groundnuts tell you so. They seem to emerge from graves of dust, painted nails, hands, feet and all singing their shrilly sunny songs.

Buy some groundnuts, sir they cry cheerily through dust-flecked teeth.

The girls faces, heavily daubed in mascara, gleamed beneath the sunlight. In between gossiping and games of hopscotch they continued to advertise their wares in high-pitched voices. Most of them chewed flavourless gum as if it was a signifier of hipness.

In those rooms, one quickly loses all notions of privacy that one had previously held. There's simply no point since one has to co-exist in peace with imposed room mates. In most instances, the experience is not unpleasant. Good friends sometimes emerge from terrible situations. But sometimes the very worst occurs. Most of the doors have no locks and property is left to the mercy of chance and thieves. At night, stray dogs condemned to the wilds come prowling through the corridors looking for rancid left-overs. One should add that there is no fence around the site to hinder intruders. The ladies are most vulnerable since their building is located at an easily accessible point. No matter, the army boys would keep them occupied.

On the throne of authority are the site administrator and commandant. The administrator is a dark pot-bellied man of medium height, a fast-talker and a veritable brown nose. He rose to his position clinging to the anus hairs (by his teeth) of his superiors remote and near. The commandant on the other hand is a short, light complexioned army captain. He is ruthless with men but with women he loses all his elements and becomes soggy cheese. It is said that he treats men harshly because he was always being sexually molested by his mates when he was at the military academy. Whatever the case may be, he never took it lightly with men. But with women, he was all smiles, all soggy beancake and butter.

Life on the site was not enjoyable for most. Rising at five or so every morning to attend morning drill amidst the inexorable buzz and pestering of flies, marching off to hear boring compulsory lectures on old fashioned themes such as patriotism and nationalism which were only occasions of mass yawning. And then afternoon drills and nightly roll-calls. All very boring no doubt. But the privates who are suppose to be your instructors tell you it's good for the discipline. Discipline? What could be more misleading? The whole site is awash with corruption from top to bottom. The personal kits that are meant to be issued to the noble servants are taken to town and sold by the officials. Government food, (astronomical by third world standards) is sold as well while the servants are fed on chaff and slops. But where does one complain, we the servants and the governors are equally soiled with the muck and grime of corruption. We just await our turns to be givers and receivers of contagion. Oh sure greed fosters the pestilential fat of the land and we as onlookers can mutter ineffectual complaints. So while noble servants of the nation went about poorly kitted, some smart city-dwellers roamed around cladded in freshly made national wears. Not to worry, those national wears were of abysmally inferior quality anyway. They only had to dipped in water for them to lose shape and colour. After about three washings, they were only fit for the bin. But some poor city-dwellers made these inferior wears a source of pride and both the old and young could be seen walking through the length and breadth of the town in their poorly crying shades. It was all part of the groove in this part of the world, a social phenomenon that was gladly accepted without much argument.

Within the camp site no one was aware of this though. No one was permitted out of those fenceless grounds without an official pass. And for a man to get a pass he had to see blood coming out of the back of his eyes but a woman only had to sleep with the right person but this wasn't always easy as well because sometimes she had to sleep with ten or so guys before she found the real man in charge. All that wasted love spilt all over the place. You needed buckets of spittle and tears to wash it all away. But soon some smart ladies found the way to beat the restriction on movement – simply allow yourself to be invited by junior military officers to their orgiastic parties which were held at regular intervals in town. Never mind about those khaki dudes pawing you all over for they were usually dim-witted. They never went as courageously for their invited sweet pants as they went for their guns which was a shame because they showered so much money and gifts in vain upon those man-eating chicks.

See ya lads ! but tell us when is the next party ? the sweet pants cry out when they leave. This frequent moonlighting by the girls caused female shortage within the site and some lads took to emergency homosexuality. In fact one day Olu Ray was going to another building to see a friend when he stumbled through a door and saw two naked muscular and handsome guys having a go at it. Fortunately, he had a camera and he asked if he could capture their most climatic moment for posterity. Gerrout or I'll give you a dirty kick in the balls.

Wonderful and he went out of the room regretting the fact that he could not record that rare visual sight. Others who were not so adventurous took to masturbation and intelligent young men could be found gathered under the trees at night with all sorts of lubricants discussing famous decadents in the most blasé tones and constructing discourses about the marvels of narcissism derived from onanism. These bright minds also discussed at great length fellatio and phallic adoration in male archetypes. It was called getting to see and know thyself without the aid of a mirror. The poets amongst them composed poems about groups of lovely dark haired mulatto men-children masturbating in huge mirrored cathedrals while their female subjects watched lost in awe for they were supposed to be gods. The females on their part sang divine songs about wanting to touch them, to hold them, to kiss them and make them issue forth with seed. The unfortunate thing was that these poems were never read outside this circle. Most of them would be lost in time while others were just left to be buried in dust. Uncaptured time and desert sands destroyed all man-made art. The incomparable poetry of the sun-drenched universe of sands could not tolerate the smallness of things made by men. Lingering images of the unfaltering splendour of the Hellenic body and mind. One of those onanistic tear-jerkers went:

> *Oh baby can I touch you?*
> *I mean really hold you,*
> *Until I become exactly like you?*
> *I cry and I cry*
> *Only for you.*

This romance-inclined poet made it known that he had smeared the page with tears. Nonetheless these non-conforming poets were the most noble-hearted amongst the servants of the land. In time their strengths would become isolated from centres of power by the greed and corruption that was flooding the land. Within the camp site, a couple of dreadlocked marijuana smokers tried to become heralds of controversy but controversy eluded them and they became objects of pity, standing but broken nonetheless because they had become suspended amid the dry vastness of time and dust.

Olu Ray drifted among the various ideological groups within the camp hoping to find a home. The homosexuals had rejected him for his thoughtlessness and insensitivity. The poets could only accept him as a second rate member on the basis of his half-hearted attempts at pessimistic poetry. He was no *poet maudit*. Even then he found the poets a bit too far out so he moved on towards the girls who were fast becoming public property when they were not completely ridden with the quest for the Lord.

Oh Christ halleluja I'm torn apart by desire he cried himself nightly to sleep.

It didn't make matters any better when Romeo the head of the poets' caucus found himself a willing muse in the person of Beatrice. However she hadn't any of the qualities Dante associated with his own muse. She was pretty alright in a worldly sort of way. She also had dark thickly flowing surreal hair but she was outright bitchy and mean. Romeo fell in love with her milky complexion. He liked to put his tongue against her skin so he could taste her lemon freshness. He read the whole of Dante again just because of her but his intelligence was over-mastered by his lust for her so he could not discover the wide divide between the Dantean Beatrice and his mulatto muse, - a situation recalling the great Baudalaire who sank into the vast lyrical depths of the evil passion, mad desire and subterranean debauchery to dredge up poetry of supreme irony for a love that all but ruined him. Still in the words of the great but unknown Romeo;

I cry and I cry for you.

A curious mix of lachrymose romanticism and tongue-in-cheek cynicism.

At night Romeo would take Beatrice through the tall pine trees, through partially concealed tracks of dust, across the small wooden makeshift bridge, down another beaten dust track, past the deserted administrative building to the desolate moonlit fountain that had a couple of stone benches around it. There, he would sing her embarrassing tear-jerkers by rock artists that she could not appreciate as she frolicked by the fountain that drank incessantly from her image. Romeo would then write poems about his eternal erections that Beatrice did nothing to heed. He would fall upon his knees under the moonlight to beg her to give him a blow job if she

10

would not make love to him and she would refuse both, touch his erection lightly and run off laughing into the dark woods. Romeo would then fantasise about having her gang raped but then his brother poets were much too soft-hearted to carry out such a thing. His brain and veins would overflow with the green sludge of sorrow. He might as well die upon a mud land littered with half-dead frogs. At least he would be able to find solace and ponderous romance in the solemn poetry of greenland death.

Back in the buildings in which they were accommodated, the less adventurous servants played loud electronic music on little tape-recorders. In the corridors, there was dancing and shuffling according to whatever groove or jam was playing. It didn't matter if one did not do it right since as soon as a beat was mastered, another took the world by storm. Revolutionary progress by total elimination. Internecine mass destruction in pursuit of a Darwinian ideal of perfection.

Music today is the art of the most opportunistic alchemist. One doesn't simply stay in one groove for so long. Look at what happened to James Brown. The great man got petrified in his dancing shoes. Electro funk-jamming-to-the-beat demands that you feed a heartless voice into a computer to screech about love in Armageddon and that's music brother, music! Don't feed on a single hype for sake of comprehension or you'll get left out in the cold so move your feet to the beat. Eat up the heat and vomit up the sweat. This is not worthy of *diabolus in musica*. The jam is up. The groove is down low.

Soon it would be time to leave the site and the noble servants would be posted to various places of work to render much-needed services. It was particularly a period of dread for most people because if one got unlucky, one could be flung into the most remote outposts where there was no electricity or water, where there were no hospitals or decent housing, where illiteracy and disease degraded the quality of life. These drawbacks were what the noble servants were supposed to conquer by aidless ingenuity. The nation would be built upon monumental bloodshed and fractured bones. From time to time there would be memorials in honour of the dead otherwise one would have to be content with work without incentive or acknowledgement.

Life on site grew bitter for the men. The girls where taken out to play by junior military officers who could not believe their good fortune. The parties in town went on and the lucky officers lost some of the stiffness in their manners (being so unaccustomed to women). The male servants, on the other hand, could only complain quietly under trees where they played games of scrabble and chess before lights out. For them, it was a life full of harsh discipline. But their bitterness was made far more acute by the fact the high-ups were not able or perhaps were unwilling to abide by the strictures of their own discipline.

One night when there was to be a party, the lads on the site found out that all the party-loving girls had been taken out to town for another gig held by the army boys. The site commandant, Leachie, pretended not to be aware and made a showing at the girlless site party to further underline his unawareness. A few of his sycophantic male assistants were dancing alone or with themselves, bone to bone. The plan was that when the rigmarole finally ended they would all hit the town for the real gig. No show definitely that night for the camp boys. All the site lads knew what was happening and decided to have a showdown. It began when some of the lads started singing lewd songs about their missing girls incriminating the commandant. For a few minutes he pretended not to hear anything until empty soft drink bottles began to be hurled through the makeshift dance hall door. It was then Leachie came out playing the soldier with his pathetic height. It was already dark and there was no moonlight so the lads could do as they wished. Darkness they say, provides a good cover for children of the night.

What's going on out here? cried Leachie with a touch of despair in his voice.

Where are all our girls or do you want to make queers of all of us?

What do mean where are your girls? In their rooms of course.

Well go up to their rooms and bring them out here, at least we are supposed to be having a party said the same fearless voice of one of the servants again.

What's that speaking?

Right here shorty, do you wanna try me?

Look gentlemen we can settle this amicably

Well you've always believed in terror said another voice in the darkness.

Now may I ask what really happened to your girls? asked Leachie ignoring the speaker and trying to sound friendly.

You should tell us since you invited all your friends to take them out.

But that's not true and in any case your girls would not have gone anywhere if they really loved you.

No one could give a good reply to the challenge and the opposition rapidly grew feeble. The lads started to shuffle their feet about and went back to their half-completed games of chess and scrabble. Leachie and his obsequious assistants went back to dancing bone to bone for a while and then hit town as was planned for the real gig.

Beatrice too went out for the party. If she didn't, who would have? The following day, she complained to Romeo that it was a lousy gig. There were lots of food and drinks alright but the army boys were awkward movers as well as drab conversationalists. They just kept putting their feet into their jaws and over their heads. A bunch of pathetic camels to put it more precisely.

Then why don't you fall for guys like me? asked Romeo imploringly.

No darling, no money, no power. Love cannot thrive without these two things nowadays she said dashing off into the dimming woods.

*****

Olu Ray did not find much luck too with the girls. He just kept agonising over his Wagnerian passions. Why was it that love hardly comes to under-achievers? His thoughts started to find form. There was truly something Machiavellian about love in the post-modern age. Love? Can it really be said to exist with all its attendant prim qualifications and hard-eyed rationalisations? The girls are lovely, yeah, truly gorgeous but they all say honey I gotta run, I'm strictly commercial now. When viewed from a strictly Situationist point of view, how dreadfully banal. So poets keep composing their tear-jerkers for the coming of another Romantic Age. With heavy hearts and sullen heads we await the re-emergence of the pre-Raphaelite soul so that we can all yawn in a rainbow-decked valley of bliss. Perhaps it is what humankind needs by way of rejuvenation.

Olu Ray was only partially successful. He met a girl Hazy. She had a terra cota complexion and an ingratiating smile. She was also slim and had a way of walking. A lot of guys were drawn to her. She freely made friends with them but she fell in love with no one. She took a liking to Olu because of his disarming passivity. Undressing before him did not cause her any discomfort. He was quite gentlemanly. Olu fell in love with her care-free nature and confessed to her. She laughed heartily and told him to forget all about it because it would only cause him unbearable torture. But how was this to be?

Love is not a switch that is turned off and on at will. Once it finds its way into the heart of a person, it spreads overwhelmingly like snake venom. The pain for Olu was beyond crying to sleep every night. He could never compose himself adequately in her before. Oh she was worse than

Lolita, she was more like a serpentine Madonna without a heart. Madonna could be associated with dark romance and the enigma of an inscrutable smirk. But verily Hazy was nothing but a sunny terror that sometimes seemed completely oblivious of its dreadful influence. Olu would spend ages in her six person tenanted room looking glum and being a nuisance for love. He became a sucker and a sorry excuse for a motherfucker. Then one day she took pity on him. She was going to influence his posting to a favourable place when they left camp. This could hardly be called sympathy or empathy. What was the point of living in loveless luxury? What was the point in having a guitar without strings? What was the point in possessing a heart that won't be shattered? Desire is such a forlorn emotion at the stage of cock-strewn postadolescence. And Olu craved Hazy more than the flesh of own body. If only she would agree to become merged with him for a few precious moments. If only he could watch over her, no, closely guard her while she slept. If only she could grant him a realistic piece of his dream of agony for the duration of his existence and then be free to continue on her endless dream journeys. If only... and he'll be satisfied. He sighed wearily and he knew within himself that it was only poetry and not reality that could capture the pseudo-Platonic transcendentalism of his love.

When Hazy told the site administrator (the pot-bellied ignoramus) about her wish to be redeployed to a much more cosmopolitan province and about Olu too being favourably located, he frowned and said there was a price for everything. She would have to sleep with him. She would have to lure other girls into the world of profitable vice. Hazy replied that was fine with her but there's also a price men had to pay with sleeping with girls. They had to be taken out. Girls, they say, like to have fun, they like to be taken out to dine sumptuously on caviar, smoked salmon and prime beef and to guzzle champagne and vintage wines. The entire works, oh you poor devils. For this is supposed to be the good life philosophers

15

through the ages have been constructing millennial systems and concepts to discover. Those fucking shit-eaters spend man-annihilating hours taking laborious roundabout approaches to find the heart of what the good life meant. All failed except the epicureans who found pleasure to be a fine principle or the hedonists who upheld sybaritic delights. But by and large, individual philosophers no matter their brilliance were always too half-hearted in embracing the simple idea of having fun or put plainly, having a good fuck. When they did, they equally found themselves dying over-simplistic deaths. This, in the main, can be attributed to their preoccupation with logocentric phenomena. How does one simply extricate oneself from the labyrinthine galaxies of the pursued word? How does one discontinue the destruction of the signified without the consequent loss of an ever-inquiring intellect? One had to perform the grand feat of having one's cake and eating it concurrently. To complete the task of over-reaching the intellect through its own very limited resources. Sounds fine, in fact Kantian viewed on the basis of its metaphysical ambitions. But the eternal question is how is it to be achieved? Why not adopt the deconstructive means of killing the notion of life just as all notions of God have been brushed aside? Instead of ruminating on the headless and tailless curd of life, one should discard that very curd and plunge into the free-flowing stream of appearance and institute a deconstruction of history beginning from the future using autochthonous processes independent of all known epistemological systems and traditional thought-processes. In other words, punk thought *in extremis* from the unknown to the familiar. The task would now be to inaugurate the Age of Probabilities with a self -regulating and self-correcting Kantian attitude. No Life, no Death, no Void. Nothing.

Every possibility would in advance predict its own birth and dying. Every span of terror would pronounce without prevarication its own self-defeating limitations. No discourse of power would be able to effect a transhistorical, transcendent impact. In this thesis is to be found a recipe by which some understanding may be gotten of the miracles and paradoxes of the future's way of rolling into history the carpet of misunderstanding and confusion. It is hoped that contained in this effort is its antithetical negation.

In the large parking lot, every night Olu Ray would sit in semi-darkness to watch his irresistible tormentor, Hazy being carried away in the site administrator's vehicle for a night of illicit lovemaking. Then, he would wish he were in the administrator's shoes without his pot-belly. He wished he rode in the administrator's car but without his lack of awareness of the perceptiveness of swishing trees that lined his path. He wished he was standing in his place without his freckles. He would watch Hazy in her pair of blue jeans singing to herself and polishing her nails at the back seat of the car. Could she at that moment entertain a care in the world? It would seem as if tears were welling up in the dim melancholy of his heart. His beauty goes out every night to lose some water from her tainted well of virtue. Rainer Maria Rilke would certainly have described it better under the dusky aura of venomous thorns. He would have heralded a multitude of diverse poetic airs into a pool bubbling with celestial symphonies of gloom, unrequited passion, unreason, loss and regret. For Olu it was as if he lost a pint of blood during every one of those nights of pain. One night when he could no longer bear it he asked the gifted Romeo to compose an elegy for his mercurial bird of the night. This was the result:

Girl of the pumpkin field
Regard how I die for you,
With a round little moon in my mouth
And oh sugar spice,
I am the one calling out to you
From dark barren country.

When Olu Ray read it, he was not very pleased. To him, it read like doggerel but what could he do? He was no poet and would never be one. He tucked the piece of paper into his pocket and went to his post to await the return of his night bird if indeed she would come back that night. She did not. He went to his cold bed mumbling to himself in lugubrious tones.

The following day, Olu Ray saw her where people gathered to play chess chatting with a group of guys. She was holding court and she looked radiant and beautiful as usual and the lads were extremely proud of her company. It shot them up immeasurably up the social scale. They all listened with rapt attention without comprehending all her words because they were too busy devouring the material symbols of her physical endowments. She relished the attention they lavished upon her like spineless lap dogs. Olu felt jealous and apprehensive as he approached the group but he knew he had better cling to remainder of his dwindling courage.

Why are you always fucking me up? he asked tonelessly when he was within earshot. She failed to heed him and it was impossible to tell whether it was deliberate or not. Olu then asked the question again after grabbing her arm. The look on her face indicated perplexity and anger at his audacity. But more of anger really.

Are you sure you're not drunk or have you smoked something you shameless boy. What an insult! What do you mean by I'm always fucking you up? Nobody fucks you up but yourself. You're not even a man, you're only a boy that's why you'll always remain fucked up! Can you believe that I go out every night with that filthy site administrator just to ensure that this ingrate does not get posted to the end of the world where he could die unmourned like the lousy monkey he that he is and he comes here with enough guts to tell me that I am fucking him up. What nerve! Alright it's finished between us and I never want to set eyes on you again.

18

She then stormed off to her room without looking back. All the lads who had gathered about her started to make fun of Olu Ray who by now was completely prostrate with shame. Though he did not smoke, he thought seriously about buying himself a cigarette but his legs failed to move. Still totally dazed he went back to the room to watch spiders spinning webs across the ceiling. He had been disgraced and the story was bound to break like wild fire in the harmattan. The myriad tongues of the wind would hurl in a helter skelter fashion innumerable tales of his abjection. It would be said that he had been dressed down by a girl and he had been unable to whimper like a badly beaten dog. After that incident, Olu Ray did not harbour any more amorous intents. Fear had gotten the better of his desires and whilst others chatted on moonlit nights with co-operative girls he watched spiders and other insects crawling upon the ceiling. Fear began to eat his soul with Hitlerian determinism. He might have been a dark, illegal Moroccan immigrant at the mercy of some old and ugly German woman.

*****

Soon the period stipulated to be used on the site ended. They were all issued letters informing them of the places in which they were to offer their services. For the whole of two days before the final day, a fever of anxiety swept through the site. Some of the lads bribed the junior officials to influence their postings. Girls who were interested in such favours had to sleep with them. They had been concentrating their efforts in wrong places. A few disappointed girls could not conceal their grief and complained to the hearing of all. They merely exposed themselves to further abuse and ridicule. People booed them. They had sold themselves cheaply for nothing, however nothing of this sort happened to girls like Beatrice and Hazy. They got redeployed to places of their dreams because they had concentrated their efforts in the right places. So on the last day such girls were full of smiles and empty kisses for their friends. Olu Ray had not been posted to an outpost of misery, poverty and disease but there was nothing to be happy about. His night bird had been redeployed so what could be his lot apart from misery and then the disease that ate into aggrieved hearts? He read his letter absent-mindedly and failed to comprehend its contents. The other noble servants were busy congratulating and consoling themselves but he carefully avoided their activities. Instead he found a tree stump to sit and brood upon. A few of his friends came to him and asked him about his luck and he handed them his letter. They congratulated him for not been taken out of the town. But was there anything to be happy about? Or was he merely dumb? He wished he could get high and then have a great big hangover. He wished he were dumber than he already was, he wished he would overdose on lithium underneath a derelict bridge where vagrants resided.

There were virtually no legal drinking bars and alcohol could only be sold illicitly in hideous looking brothels and other Islamised dens of iniquity where marijuana was smoked freely. And needless to say such grotto-like places were always open to ruthless police raids in which both the innocent and guilty were lumped together. He longed for a place where he could enjoy his beer with a regular heart beat, where he didn't have to look fearfully over his shoulder every other minute like some cornered animal. It was difficult to understand what the congratulations were all about in this place which was another country without his faithless Hazy to console him.

Trucks were brought to convey some of the noble servants to their destinations. Olu watched listlessly as his colleagues hurled their stuff into the vehicles. He did not even bother to get a few addresses. The irrevocable loss of Hazy was all that occupied him. Moments later it started to rain heavily. People started to run for cover and he too wearily walked into a roofed void beside the camp mosque.

He watched the rain fall into the soup pots of the women who sold food in the open. Some of them had thatched roofs over their sheds but they did little to prevent the rain. The ground within their sheds was soon soaked and marshy. Still people streamed in to buy food. To many it was a good idea because no one knew when they would eat next. Olu Ray wasn't hungry but he knew he too had to eat something because it seemed a good idea. However, he decided he would wait until the crowd had dispersed.

Half an hour later, he went into one of the typhoid-plagued eating joints and ordered some food. The shed had about three people still eating and the two tables had not been cleared. There were many dirty dishes that made the shack uninviting. The tables and thatched roofs also had water running off their edges. Olu Ray told one of the waitresses to clean up the mess but she was too busy trying to attract other customers to hear him. He gave up in utter frustration. When she finally decided to serve him, she spooned up a minted coin from the pot of soup and Olu just told her to forget about it all and started to walk away. She called at him to pay for the already dished out meal but he neglected to heed her. She was angered that her efforts over him were wasted. Olu was mildly astonished by the stupidity of her audacity. There was no need for him to fret over her bullshit. He walked to another shed and waited while the serving girls attended to their customers. They only had pounded yam. Inside the shed, there were two medium-sized benches that were soaking wet. None of the girls did anything to wipe off the running water. A few customers sat pathetically eating their meals, while others waited impatiently for them to finish. Olu cut a picture of supreme indifference. He wasn't looking forward to eating in the water-logged shed that had a deluge of flies. The food too looked horrid. But what could he do? He couldn't narcoticise or get a hangover. Was he plain dumb then? Only death by heroin or the gun could tell. He would just eat his meal mechanically and then

21

vacate the shed. When it was his turn to be served, the last batch of pounded yam was finished. For a few moments, Olu stood looking about abjectly and then walked away to try his luck at some other shack.

He came to another shed where they were draining some excess water from a potful of boiled rice and he decided to wait there. There were a few other people waiting and they all watched the women as they started making preparations to wash the dirty dishes. The customers stood on muddy ground watching as if they were participants in a séance. As one of the waitresses finished washing a plate, she handed it over indiscriminately to the most aggressive customer. Olu Ray was not interested in being aggressive and so he was one of the last to receive a plate. The struggle for spoons and forks was even fiercer and this time Olu Ray almost lost out to a short thick set girl who had a notorious mouth. She eyed him in a mean way as he snatched the fork just before her. In fact he was to have gotten the fork first but she took a shameless dive for it. Anyway Olu had gotten it before her so she just chilled and waited like an aggrieved leopard for another try.

The guys had come to realise that there was no use in playing the gentleman because you stood to lose. So much for social decorum. Olu Ray stood eating his meal slowly under a tree that was dripping with rain-water like the rest of the baleful little crowd. No one complains in blind country where sellers are kings and queens. You took what you were given gratefully and hoped passively for a better day. You begged to be given a right and then backed off into the stink of shadows until you were called forth with supplicant arms and a bowed head. Contentment is a very difficult condition to achieve, there was something definitely sagacious about it but Olu's state, all the same, may be called the reverse side of contentment because it was tinted by an almost criminal indifference. He was a less erudite, less rigorous sort of a junk thought creep who wished to live out the entire span of his life in the toxic aftermath of an irreparably ruined tropical paradise. Paradise? Yes in times before history had a name. Before the loss of edenic innocence, paradise seemed entirely possible.

Olu finished his meal and put down his plate carefully on the floor and went back to the void beside the mosque where he had kept his stuff. He wasn't looking forward to anything and he did not mind playing the aimless vagabond. Slowly, he walked toward the camp gate. By now the site was fairly deserted. The next logical step would have been for him to report at his place of work but the numbing passivity that plagued him did not compel him to do so.

When he got past the gate he saw motorbikers looking for passengers to convey to town. Motorcycles were the main source of transportation in the town. The bikers hardly spoke English. One had to communicate with a rudimentary form of sign language. Olu felt like sight-seeing just as a proper tourist. After walking for almost a kilometre, the heat of the sun made him change his mind. Perfunctorily he waved down a motorbiker and got on the machine. When he was asked where his destination was, he just pointed straight ahead. The biker nodded and sped on. After all he was only after money. It was a good thing that Olu was in uniform. People in the town viewed all noble servants with respect. As they sped on, little children waved cheerfully at him. He merely nodded back at them. He soon began to think seriously about where he should make his destination. The problem was solved when he saw a fellow noble servant walking towards the town centre. He made the biker stop by the guy and paid his fare. Walking toward his unknown colleague, he said hello. Hi the servant replied cheerfully.

It was always a consolation to meet another fellow traveller on strange land. Folks are strange and you are lonely. Folks are strange and they make tiger faces at you. Shit gets strange when folks take photographs of you when you are upside down walking on the ceiling in a pretty model's flat. Shit gets serious when you open your veins and bleed into the

23

wound of the one you think you love. In Egypt of the magicians, shit and folks are strange when death and the lyric copulate in a resurrected blaze of decadent flowers. Shit is strange. Folks are fucked.

There were virtually no high rise buildings at the town centre. The road they were walking on was a commercial one. They started to talk about the ill luck that had brought them to what they regarded as god-forsaken country. They told themselves about the relatively happy lives they led back in their homes. About the lovely girl friends they left behind. At intervals, they would both lapse into silence over their cherished reminiscences. Hugo, for that was the name of his friend, had an Adam's apple that throbbed when he thought hard about the past he had left behind. He too hadn't been to his place of work and also felt like roaming about the small town. It was said that one could get around the whole place on a motorbike in about an hour. Small place really, but it had such a big name just as a small name disease with a seismic bang.

They continued to roam about until sun-set and then they started feeling hungry. As they walked on, they came across a long line of cheap eating kiosks that sold familiar food. They went into one of them that had a squalid interior- broken window frames, cracked cement here and there, empty plastic bottles and besmeared cellophane on the floor- and ordered some solid food. It took some time in coming and so they ordered two bottles of Seven-Up and did some more listless chatting. When their meals were finally brought, Hugo ate with some relish while Olu Ray ate slowly. After he finished, Hugo got up pay for both meals surprising Olu who was easily astonished by human kindness. Misanthropy produces common seductions.

It was past five o' clock when they carried their bags and ventured onwards. It also occurred to them that they had no place to sleep for the night. Hugo suggested that they walk towards the district office of the noble servants' bureau. To

24

Olu, it was not a bad idea. Anyway he had no choice. As they went on, a herd of cattle crossed the street stopping the moving traffic. This Africa you know. Shit creeps out of the jungle and lands straight atop the tables of five star hotels. Such sights were common and cattle are the unquestioned lords of the road. I agree to be called a cow in order to get a hand-out from you. In other words, I agree to kiss your arse.

Being a predominantly Islamic town, small prayer grounds were to be found every where. Almost every street corner had one. Motorists would alight from their vehicles to observe the call to prayer. Pedestrians were free to stop at the next convenient prayer ground to worship Allah. One did not see too many women going about aimlessly. Most of them were kept in purdah. And on the entrances of many houses was a boldly printed instruction; DON'T ENTER. It was even said within the town that a man cannot venture into the interior of his brother's house without express permission which was hardly ever given. Instead, he had to wait outside while his brother came to meet him. This piece of information sent a chill down Olu's spine. He vowed to himself not to even look twice at the door on which such a frightening notice was pasted. But gee, the women, when one got to see them were so beautiful. They were demure and submissive beings who submitted the care of their souls to the Almighty Allah and the custodians of their meek and veiled bodies were their husbands. Olu could not help but agree that God is great after thinking about this societal set-up. But how on earth was he to satisfy his irrepressible longing for female company in a town that believed completely in sexual segregation even as the entire world sped through the twenty first century? How could a man sit beside the fountain and altar of womanhood to pay his dues to nature with frightful notices dotting everywhere like spectres? And the worst part of all was that one had to endue this enforced celibacy for a period of one full year. And the women come and go wearing thick opaque veils. And the women come and go perfumeless. Don't worry Michelangelo won't come home. Olu's heart sank and he bit his lips bitterly.

When they finally reached the district offices, the rays of the sun had totally disappeared. Outside, seated under a lushly leaved tree, were fellow noble servants who were passing the time chatting to conceal their misery and hapless fate. Littered around were travelling bags and suitcases. There was no space left on the few benches around so Olu and Hugo stood standing. A plump light complexioned girl started to complain;

This country is so fucked up! They bring us out to this god-forsaken shithole saying they need our services only to neglect us. After all we are some of the best minds in the country and the country's leaders bring us here to rot not caring a fuck about our welfare or well-being. Is this how a great nation treats its citizens? We complain daily about dependence, insufficiency and mismanagement but we all know where the vices begin. We all know how we bleed ourselves daily using our own knives. Here we are now languishing in total abandonment when there are supposed to be government officials to minister to our needs, to store up our ebbing morale, but where are those bloody officials now? Oh they are busy embezzling funds, the miserable allowances that are meant for us while we are supposed to starve like unwanted dogs! As for me if the country does not require my services, I'm ready to go back into the bosom of my loving family.

When she finished everyone nodded their heads in agreement with her. Others soon picked up the threads of her thinking and developed them along other lines. Olu listened carefully to all that was said but said very little himself. Hugo on the other hand made his presence felt with his witty contributions.

The main entrance to the office was still open and in the lobby, there were a number of spare mattresses. Some of the noble servants started to bring them out for the night because it was time to lock up the entrance. It had only being left open because many servants were milling around. There were not enough mattresses to go around and Hugo and Olu had to share a thin worn-out one. Gradually, a desert chill started to creep up and some people began to shiver. Those who had blankets in their bags brought them out and covered up themselves. Neither Hugo nor Olu had one so they got ready to brace the cold. The chill however was not the only problem. A swarm of mosquitoes had been hovering above and had began to descend in droves. Everyone knew they were in for a bitter night. The hard gravelly ground did not help matters and Hugo and Olu being fairly big guys had it particularly rough.

A little away from the trees, under the car porch, a bunch of born-again Christians were getting ready for a long night of prayers, clapping, exhortations, singing and speaking in tongues. They had started to proclaim fervently that sweet Jesus would see them through the night and be with them for all eternity. Olu looked into their midst and saw that they were mainly women. They looked prim and proper, a trifle too strung up to be approached in a worldly manner. So he just kept his cool and looked into the starless sky. It was a thick black night. Shortly afterwards, Hugo started to snore. Olu found it amazing that Hugo found sleep so easily in spite of the enveloping roughness. Olu Ray found the night one of the harshest he had ever known. The mosquitoes made his nostrils catacombs for their escapades. They flew into his ear lobes and made distressing music. They entered his clothes through small openings and drew unholy draughts of blood. For him, sleep wouldn't just come.

His strong abiding hatred for mosquitoes made it impossible to sleep. Later, he got up and went to where the born-again Christians were praying with frenzied motions. He stamped his feet into the ground with a bowed head. It seemed like he was praying but the fact was that he wasn't.

He was slightly disgusted by his own subterfuge. But he was also glad no one bothered with him. When a woman asked if there was anyone present who wanted to give their life to Christ, Olu remained silent with his head bowed. He had long since lost all longing for religion, eternity or immortality. Although he was a person with somewhat spiritual sympathies, he had lost the strength for the nurturing of faith. Faith had a hard, blind unyielding core as well as an uncritical innocence. Life had exposed him to the sarcasm of worldly devilry and beserkry. A foxy sort of cunning that was able to heap scorn upon itself, to grin at itself, one that was able to say come, cut out the crap, you know you're so full of shit so don't pretend to be what you're not. People who observed him carefully were able to discern this attitude clinging about his person. What made sense to him were mind-numbing sessions of primal scream therapy, heavy-bearded beatnik riffs, consciousness altering mind-games, elaborate and ritualised communal mind-fucks, Fluxus cut-up lyrics, minimalist wall of sound, Biafra and Bangladesh. It was time to give religion a big bloody one up the arse, it was time to usher Nietzsche through the dark void with a large cigar dangling from his lips to deliberate upon a perennially absent God and the plague of syphilis.

And so as the Babel-tongued sisters poured forth their Esperanto, Olu sat stamping his feet into the ground to chase away the mosquitoes although it may have looked as if he was praying or admonishing demons. He did not have the moral strength to ask God to drive off the merciless mosquitoes even though he sometimes made half-hearted calls upon the Lord when in distress. We all do if for instance, we sense the imminence of a ghastly accident. We yell Jesus even though we avoid the name in stable times. Hypocrisy is a true cancer of the spirit.

As dawn approached, the prayers ceased and the small circle of the children of Jesus started to introduce themselves to one another. Olu gladly participated in these routinised introductions. It was always cheerful to have someone with whom to exchange a few words after a sleepless night. Although he was careful not to reveal too much about himself so that he wouldn't later feel unnecessarily obliged. The chatting was alright except that it was marred by excessive politeness which hinders easy-going familiarity together with a real communion of spirits; sister this, sister that, brother this, brother that. All those religious pleasantries he found quite constricting. He preferred more direct ways of expressing togetherness. Hi brother man! How are you doing! What's up with you and so on and forth. I got the funk man, how about you? It is time to dance away from the chains of our constrictions, oh freaky me, I'm knee-deep in the universal groove, I'm ready to boogie while the wolf among the haystacks howls at the moon, yeah, the killing floor is besmeared with dancehall blood, I've been stung up the arse by acid, the spirit of Syd Barrett lives! He felt through such ways, one could tell exactly where everyone else was at. But who was he to legislate how people saluted one another? Every social setting had its peculiar set of rules and beliefs and if one did not agree with a certain way of doing things one could always move on.

Some people started to go about brushing their teeth and washing their hands and faces with chilled water. Olu found it was a wise way to keep distracting the seemingly endless deluge of mosquitoes. Hugo hadn't still woken up. It was simply amazing how he could sleep under such terrible conditions. After washing up, Olu came and sat by his friend to chase away blankets of reeling mosquitoes. It kept him occupied for a while. Hugo opened his eyes for a few moments and looked at his friend with a vague, slumberous curiosity and then drifted back into sleep.

When it was bright enough and Hugo could no longer sleep amid the buzz of morning activity, he got up, stretched out himself and had a long yawn. Soon flies would take over from the mosquitoes. Some joked about his having been able to sleep so deeply in spite of the harshness of the terrain. One person even went as far as asking him whether he had been to jail before. There, one learnt to sleep in a little cell filled with more than say twenty two people all stinking terribly with unwashed bodies amid numerous puddles of urine. Hugo hadn't been to prison but there was no point replying the cruel joke, the day was bound to throw in more than enough challenges to be answered. He gave the sky a hard thoughtful gaze and yawned again. He then blinked fast a few times as if to make himself more alert. It was then that he came to total consciousness. Slowly, he got up and went to the water pump that stood at the other end of the premises to wash his face and brush his teeth. No one bothered to change their clothes. The khaki material suited everyone since it was meant to withstand harsh conditions. Soon after, the mattresses were taken inside underneath a central stairway that went all the way up the building. Many started to complain about having had horrible nights. But this was to be expected. Even in discomfort, comfort is always being sought after. Survival is another name for it.

It was now left to see how they would make use of the day. And it was easy to become totally hindered by inertia in the face of so many difficulties and unnecessary obstacles. For this part, Olu Ray would not have minded sitting all day looking at the face of the sun and doing nothing but the presence of Hugo made this impossible. Hugo was anxious to know what the day held in store for him. Oh boy let's go he said merrily after he had finished cleaning up and they carried their bags and moved in the direction of the town centre. Hugo thought it would be a good idea if they bought some food. Olu Ray concurred but he did not want to eat again in the place they had eaten the day before and so they moved on until they saw some southern women selling food in the open front of a huge complex of government offices. Their spirits rose from thinking they were about to eat some warm familiar food. The table at which they sat was in fact a discarded wooden box. The legs of one of the two benches was about to give way so it creaked and swayed. The legs were caked with dried mud. As they sat down, a rush of dust sprayed their way carried by a whipping wind. They looked at each other and nodded and wondered how they were supposed to eat under such circumstances. There was no point in complaining as instinct told them that they had to live for the time being on the basis of trial and error. Gathered about, were a pack of filthy boys who looked like street urchins but were not. They waited around and grabbed bowls in order to devour leftovers when customers had finished eating.

Hugo was nauseated by their sight and waved them away only for them to regroup each time like vultures and hyenas. Olu Ray could discern an insatiable hunger that crawled on the dusty faces of the menacing brats. Their deplorable plight was an extension of ill-planned government socio-economic policies which perpetuated the benefits of an almost oligarchic minority over an ever-growing mass of suffering and dispossessed souls. He was not very conversant with Karl Marx but he did not also need to learn from the social theorist that government officials in high places drew up their long and short term development plans strictly motivated by self-interest. He was sure that he was living in sub-Machiavellian times. Indeed entire generations rose to meet the struggle of life without the aid of visionary and selfless leadership and most of them were routed along the way. Olu scrutinised the faces of the boys to see any tell-tale sign of abject misery. It was difficult to see any as they all seemed to derive a primal joy from scrambling to exist on the remnants left by total strangers. It was this activity that they made up for their life's struggle- a sub-Hobbesian scramble for crumbs, bare life and breath. The stark squalor of their lives might indeed rob their struggle of the benefit of mobility and foresight but what had such lofty ideals got to do with the politics of the stomach? The fierce battle of topmost politicians over the politics of the stomach validated it as the ultimate war. Even the finest of minds sometimes yield to its humiliating temptations and ruthless ravages. And there were no revolutionaries equipped enough to guide this young starving mass towards a higher form of struggle. A struggle that would mean snatching the instruments of power from bloodied hands and entrusting them to more worthy hands. This great task requires a rare kind of strength, a steady and continuous motion towards a cherished ideal that had to be snatched from the bowels of a lost colonial past. Olu didn't always think in terms of blood-letting imagery, rather he preferred gradual but progressive transformations beginning from the dick to the arse. He believed in a commonsensical harnessing of the material and non-material attributes of available energies for the task of climbing onto a higher plane of limbo. He found this way more exacting since nothing is left to chance as is the case with mob fury. The task would be to subject the body and mind to total and effective control to accomplish some serious revolutionary shit. One can imagine the difficulties involved.

*****

After they had finished eating, the two young men tossed their plastic plates to the boys who stood like hyenas about them. As to be expected, it was the stronger ones amongst them who got the chewed upon, saliva-besmirched bits and pieces of food. They walked past an array of other food sellers, soft drink sellers, cigarette stalls and roast meat stands most of which had smoke drifting away from them. Slowly, they went their way observing the small traders with some amount of curiosity. By then, the sun was fully up and soon they were bathed in perspiration. As usual, the traffic was lackadaisical and donkey riders strode past them. Donkeys were still a widely used means of transportation for many who could not afford the luxury of a motorcar or motorcycle.

Children who had donkeys of their own felt proud and were looked upon with envy by their mates. And then they saw an even more astonishing sight – phalanxes of riders on camel back borne by a listless apocalypse of dust. They both gave a wide berth to the camels and kept looking back over their shoulders in awe. It was then they really believed they were right within the heart of the desert. Without much thought, they decided to head for the central market and then asked for the directions from a passerby who spoke English. The market happened to be a busy one and had plenty of groundnut peddlers and of course, the inevitable sugarcane and carrot sellers. People sold lots of other local delicacies in addition to different types of edible oils and palm-oil. There were tailors who were busy cutting, sewing and also engaged in the high art of embroidery. There were also stalls that sold imported wears, perfumes and exquisite body care products. And gee! the women that came to the shops. They were simply so beautiful. Most of them wore long unimaginative dresses that gave away nothing to the imagination. Olu Ray was always nearly bumping into things whilst feeding his sight. And the women looked so coy, so engrossed in what they were doing. They seemed not to speak at all. Absolute zombies in beauty land. And so Olu Ray discovered that the market place was where one could see many purdahed women.

They both got tired of seeing the market and decided to look for legal beer selling establishments. It was said that there were some on the other side of town. Two passing motorbikers were flagged down and asked to take them to where alcohol was sold and they both immediately understood. It was a long dusty ride to the place. It was mentioned that the place closed at ten o' clock every night so as not to offend the Islamic sensibilities of the town's muslim majority. No big deal. They would both swill a beer each and would not be caught dead there any time from nine o 'clock.

At any rate, it was still blazing noon and they had a lot of time to waste languishing over a couple of miserable beers.

The place, as both men now called the many rows of beer selling booths was a major landmark of non-conformism if not crossed-eyed, wild-haired bohemianism within the ostensibly alcohol-shunning town. There were also sects practicing dreadlocked Rastafarianism, plant and herb worship, invocations of the spirits of departed ancestors, back-to-the-land philosophies, underground ideologies of blackness and the adoration of menstrual blood. There were sects devoted to the cult of death. These were the fringes where autonomy was to be found. Here, marginal identities sang of the glories of particularism and the crassness of universalism. Here, the meaning and purpose of death are transmogrified; death grants his power to those who embrace him, who feed him with flesh and blood. Death transforms life into a counterfeit. The so-called living are nothing but zombies digging innumerable graves that are called rules and regulations. The degenerates that are hurled into the fringes of society glow with fierce sunlight and cackle with the boundless energies of madness. Death welcomes them to his arch chamber and lays them a feast of fresh babies. On their necks are garlands of bones. At each exhalation of breath they make, the dead rise and dance on the flat face of the moon. The moon is impregnated and in a matter of days gives birth to a million headless daughters. The cycle resumes its interminable argument.

Most of the stalls were painted red and white with Coca-Cola trademarks on them. The aroma of deep southern food wafted out some of them but it was the implacable smell of booze that hung most noticeably in the air- forbidden and defiant. As they walked on, a few burly men sat drinking outside the doors of some of the booths and were talking in rough tones. They looked like rough-looking mercenaries.

Olu found some of the stalls inviting especially the freshly painted ones but Hugo urged that they went on since there were other areas to explore within the place. However, they did not carry on their exploration to the edges of the place because Hugo at last decided to enter a shack that begun to show signs of decrepitude. Olu could not understand why Hugo would want to sit in such an ugly place. He would soon discover that a shitty joint was not always tantamount to a cheerless shithole. First of all, the woman who appeared to own the stall was fairly young although very much on the plump side. She had short hair and a face that indicated she knew how to minister to the needs of men. She knew how to butter up their coarse egos. And both Hugo and Olu Ray appeared to be fine specimens of young men. She welcomed them and had them sit on a couple of frayed armchairs within the dim seedy-looking interior that had the appearance of a brothel parlour. When they ordered for the most expensive brands of beer available, she came to hold them in greater esteem. She promptly fished out two bottles of beer and then made a small ceremony of opening and serving out their contents. Olu could see clearly her robust cleavage. She was versed in the art of giving men the ants in the sore spots of the crotch. Both Hugo and Olu pretended to be uninterested in her carefully deployed charms. This was done in gentlemanly manner so as not to give offense. They started to talk about casual matters while the young proprietress went to try her charms on two new customers who had just come in. It happened that she was quite familiar with them and she immediately engaged them in a conversation after she had brought them drinks.

Then two young ladies carrying a large portable tape recorder came in. It was the type of contraption called a ghetto blaster. They turned out to be relatives of the proprietress. The tape recorder was plugged in and the sounds emerged. The music was a mix of electro-funk and straight dance grooves and the young ladies began to gyrate encouraging each other during their solo displays to the accompaniment of the cheering men who shouted "woo

woo". It was certain that the dancing girls were bent on creating the impression they were great party freaks. One of them had a striking resemblance to the proprietress. She also had short, permed hair with a trendy cut. The other girl who was good looking was light complexioned with a lush mane of processed hair. There was something about her aura that made her seem inconsiderate. She seemed like most beautiful women to be aware of her beauty and took all the benefits that came her way as her inalienable rights – *I am beautiful hence men must attend to my demands.* Although she was fashionably dressed her clothing was inexpensive. Both girls knew the men who were cheering them on but Hugo and Olu got the feeling that they were trying to attract them. But for some reason or the other, they appeared to be more interested in their talk and their beers. After they finished their drinks, they got up to go and the proprietress came over to receive the money and bid them goodbye. She hoped they would come back regularly. To her, they appeared to be gentlemanly and composed. They both smiled courteously at her in return for her beaming grin and waved as they stepped into the waning sunlight.

There didn't seem to be any point roaming about town anymore so they decide to go back to the outdoor spot they had slept the previous night. After trekking for a while, they hailed a couple of bikers to convey them to the offices they had turned into their temporary abode. The officials were about closing for the day when they got there. Many of the noble servants could be seen accosting them with their numerous complaints. The officials on their part looked tired, bored and corrupted by the vices that usually plagued most government agencies. They couldn't just be bothered to do what they were being paid to do. Rather, they were much more interested in getting the noble servants to bribe them for inconsequential favours. The revenues derived from this illegal racket provided the mainstay for the young men who had worked there and had become bloated from feeding on many ill-gotten gains. Their cheeks swelled like puff adders when they talked or coughed. Many also received sexual favours from young ladies who came frequently asking for their assistance. No one spared, you had to pay for every small service that you were legally entitled. The net of corruption had been flung wide like an invincible succubus drawing all and sundry within its glutinous clutches. Hugo and Olu watched the open horse-trading and trade by barter. Everyone seemed to be complaining, everyone seemed to have a sad story to tell. In addition, all who gathered underneath the tree in front of the building were in for another bitter night.

The two young friends took their seats after they had settled their bags where they felt they were safe. The sun was now setting. Hugo called Olu's attention to two dust-covered figures approaching from behind. Their faded profiles looked exhausted and it turned out that one of them was a woman. She stumbled as they drew nearer and some people rushed to her to provide her some support. The young man by her side kept approaching looking rather stony-eyed. His hair was white with dust and the white vest he had on underneath his khaki had become brown with dirt and grime. Spaces were created for them to sit. The man was ushered to a tree stump and the young woman feeling uncomfortable with her sitting position, stretched out on the bench. Her breathing was heavy and laboured. She had unbuttoned her khaki top and exposed the vest she wore underneath. They were given water in large plastic cups which the woman drank spilling some out of the corners of her mouth. She resumed her panting. The man left his cup untouched and continued to gaze in front of him, stony-eyed, tight-lipped, motionless. People started to ask them all sorts of questions. The questions were directed at man since he was the stronger of the two. He ignored them for a few moments and then he began to speak as if only half-aware of those present. Still looking stony-eyed: We are returning from hell. Perhaps hell is too strong a word for it but for me I have never had to go to a place like that. It is a hamlet close to the northwestern border. We were posted to a hamlet that has no electricity or portable drinking water. I should tell you my name before I go on. I am Dan and my colleague, our colleague, I beg your pardon is Stella. I think of myself as being a failed poet. I content myself now with small revelations about the sorrowful plight of humanity in the style of beatnik sages. I hope, I hope. Anyway, to get back to my story. We went to our posts with pure hearts. I for one was glad about being posted to serve in an undeveloped locale. I looked forward to planting my own crops, growing my own food because I learnt that there was no market in the place. This is to show you how determined I was to stick it out there in that isolated cauldron of underdevelopment. While a lot of our colleagues who had been posted to similar dreary zones came back to bribe those filthy officials to have themselves re-posted to better zones I made up my mind together with Stella to endure the harshness of the land and the biting climate. I thought the unfamiliar surroundings would inspire me to write something really worthwhile. I thought if I devoted myself to the earth she would grant me her fruits and her yield a thousandfold. In my mind, I wanted the most difficult place so that I could receive strength and grow. Holding Stella's hand we boarded a broken-down truck that was heading towards our destination. We had been told it would take us there. There were in fact no buses directly plying the route. You had to walk about four kilometres on a dirt road to get to where you could get another vehicle. But when we got there, there was no vehicle. All the buses were faulty so we had to walk for another twenty five kilometres the following day. I'm sure I don't have to provide you with a complete catalogue of our sufferings, your imaginations would do just fine. When we arrived at the hamlet that day, we were like two forsaken apparitions stumbling through a dusty tract of Mephistophelean gloom. Like a scene out of Macbeth and the

38

witches. Only that this was for real. Haggard and buried in dust we appeared before the hamlet where children refused to go to school. The first people we saw shunned us as if we were ghosts but they themselves were looking like discarded relics of a lost civilization. Eventually, we got to the village well and a good Samaritan drew up a bucket of water and when he dipped a tin cup into it and gave it to me, there are worms and tadpoles swimming in the water. I asked him if this was what they all drank and of course he could not understand. There and then I turned back walking another twenty five kilometres through a gehenna of dust. So you'll understand when I tell you I have been to hell and back. I cannot praise Stella's courage and endurance enough. I had tears in my eyes all the way. This, you'll understand is well beyond tears. I was crying through relentless mists of dust with death-hugging spittle drying up at the corners of my mouth.

Throughout the narration, his voice was calm and even in tone, his facial expression deadpan. There was a long silence afterwards. Everyone seemed struck beyond words. Most obviously sympathised with them but within himself Dan felt a pang or two of guilt and shame. He removed his boots and stretched on a mattress that was provided for him on the ground. For a few minutes, he continued to stare into the sky and shortly afterwards he was fast asleep completely overtaken by exhaustion. The born-again Christian sisters began to praise the Lord and interpreted the latest testimony as an undisputable manifestation of His powers. Some went on even to hail Dan as a prophetic messenger. They pleaded with him the following morning to give his life to Christ so that he be granted the divine privilege of being amongst the elect of God. On that night, many souls became born-again Christians and there was a lot of apostolic singing and praising of the Lord.

Hugo and Olu Ray avoided the night's religious activities. The former had nothing but scorn for the religious women.

And so they went on for a long walk into the night. It felt pleasant that the moon was shining. The street they decided to take their walk had many shops some of which were still operating. Above most of the shops were billboards displaying their names. Many also had torn canopies that extended to the lip of the road. At night, the road looked like a red-light district but nothing could be more misleading. What created this false impression was probably the commercial activity going on under the red neon lights that fell onto the street. Olu was thirsty and persuaded his friend to have a soft drink with him. As they were having their drinks a storm began brewing. A strong wind whipped raging clouds of dust and people began to dash for cover underneath shredded shop canopies. Fortunately, the shop where the two friends decided to have their drinks had a canopy although it had many holes so trickles of rain water poured in. They hoped the pelting rain would stop soon but time was to prove them wrong. While it was raining they chatted with the shop-boy who seemed cheerful enough and wanted them to stay as long as they wished. They knew they could not because there wasn't enough space both within and outside the shop. They were simply too many soft-drink crates hindering easy movement and constituting obstacles to comfort. Soon enough, sizeable puddles had been created around their feet wetting their shoddy boots. There was no point in hanging around waiting for an implacable rain to stop so they decided to make a dash for it at the first opportunity. It came when a taxi-cab pulled up by the curb beside the shop that had been providing them with shelter. They immediately rushed out to meet the driver who seemed to have a warm, human face in spite of his haggard features. Without waiting to agree on the fare they hopped into the cab and asked the driver to name his price and move. It was a battered cab, a veritable junkyard piece but the equally broken-down man who drove it could obviously not afford to scrap it. It was so bad that it had no windscreen and most of the side windows were broken too. And when it moved, it tilted slightly sideways making a scrapyard cacophony. The driver, when engaged in conversation by the young men began to complain about how difficult it was to survive in view of the strangulating economic stringencies in a mild-natured way. He said he had twelve kids and a wife to feed and that life wasn't easy at all. It wasn't difficult to see that he had been sleeping rough and that the rain of easy money failed to fall upon his household. He was slowly being buried underneath a harsh country of dust with dried tears and spittle all over his face and a mocking wind tore at his shrivelled bones. He was destined to go down his valley of sorrow without the accompaniment of a gentle and fragrant gale. When Hugo and Olu saw his well-worn clothes had many holes in them, they agreed that he must be really suffering but could not understand why he decided to have as many as twelve kids. Hugo put the question to him and also asked if he didn't know about any means of contraception and the man replied that he had heard about such methods but he was unwilling to try them because he did not want to damage his wife's sexual organs. Hugo and Olu Ray looked at each other with amazement. Soon, they got to the bureau and as usual there were already mattresses spread about underneath the tree. The rain had stopped as suddenly as it had begun. A few new faces were lying about and this had the effect of making the situation worse; problems for an irrevocably corrupt establishment. Or so were the homeless victims saying. Both men were lucky to find a spare mattress which they brought up to a vacant space. Many were chatting because they found it difficult to sleep amid so many stampeding mosquitoes. As usual, the born-again Christian women were singing praises to the Lord with their frayed brightly coloured scarves. They all seemed to look the same, talked the same way, wore the same kind of clothes, and presented the same idyll of expectation only they could understand. Whenever one was privileged to hear one of them preach, one got the unmistakable feeling that the Kingdom of God was certain to bloom into realisation the next morning. They invariably beamed when spreading the gospel with an otherworldly euphoria, they offered a fascinating denial of material reality. Being part of the filth and shit, they negated it and in such a state of denial, they enjoyed the inexplicable glories of faith. Olu found one or two similarities between this kind of denial and the obviously more destructive kind present amongst users of hard drugs. It was simply time to sleep.

*****

Like the previous nights, sleep did not come to Olu but meanwhile his friend, Hugo was snoring as usual. Olu found it difficult to understand his friend's mysterious gift. The way he slept was unusual with his hands deeply tucked away in his pockets and he remained that way throughout the long cold night. On that night a dream was floating about on the quietly murmuring wind looking for a dreamer. It was a dream that sprang from the depths of inconsolable suffering, a tale that found its medium through the most unassuming telepathy, through a superlative innocence and with a spartan detachment. A ball of wind rolled into Olu Ray's ears and he knew that the men who had voluntarily submitted their beings to the god of suffering without fear or the least reservation were calling out to him. He had left them behind without saying farewell and now they had come to remind him of their existence and their daily worship of the goddess of misfortune. They, with their mute all-seeing eyes and all suffering souls had predicted he would leave them unceremoniously and he had sworn that this would not happen and now the worst had come to pass. These mysterious men were for Olu the best men in the world and he had made a pledge to himself that he would document their plight for all peoples to know. They possessed the souls

42

of sages and the hearts of truly great warriors who can now only haunt our memories. Everyday of their honourable lives was devoted to the most degrading kind of work and never did any of them complain to Olu and never did he once hear them murmuring in bitterness amongst themselves.

These noble men lived by cleaning decrepit public toilets that were never repaired and were always in use. Each day, before the sun rose, they were hard at work forcing down putrescent wastes down the drain. Olu Ray found some of them to be more intelligent than professors and their endurance firmer than world class athletes. They would carry iron buckets of shit over long distances in doing their job at a brisk pace. Olu came to be quite friendly with one of them called Otufa the Bulldozer. And it was Olu who in fact gave him the nickname " Bulldozer" out of a fondness for him and respect for his powers of endurance. He found Otufa particularly intelligent because he seemed able to make many profound statements in cryptic Nietzschean aphorisms. For instance, when Olu asked him why he didn't look for happiness elsewhere? He replied that if he did so who would bear all the sadness and suffering? He would tell witty parables about the virtues of contentment. Sometimes he would play the role of the wife and encourage Olu to play that of the husband and in this manner his invaluable lessons would be given without the least thought for reward. Olu would receive in a matter of hours knowledge the greatest minds have agonised over in endless streams of paper. Olu would ponder the various gradations of these moral lessons in his reveries. When he got up to go, he would walk on as if in haze with a revitalised spirit. At that moment, nothing remained in the sanctuary created by Otufa except the immortal words of the Bulldozer himself. Otufa took him like a son yet he treated Olu with an almost disarming deference. Sometimes Olu would want to stay longer than usual and then the Bulldozer would compare knowledge to a woman or a piece of fruit, one had to enjoy them sensibly and sparingly so as to make the pleasures derived from them more satisfying and more lasting. Otufa was also blessed with immense physical resources. He usually wore a white vest that had become brown with dirt atop a pair of blue tight fitting shorts. The bulge in his crotch was always noticeable when he wore those shorts. He wore no shoes as he made his trips to the public pump and back carrying two large pales of water in each hand. While his co-workers wore protective gloves to force excrement down the drains, he preferred to use his bare hands in doing the job. The best imagination cannot convey the horrid and nauseating state of the toilets these men washed daily. Because the drains had been blocked, shit quickly filled up the bowls to the brim and at night, rats came to feed on it. It was dreadful to see rats wallowing in the muck at dawn, stuffed with shit and ready to burst. A bad way to start the day was to see rats stuffed to the seams with human waste. Rats full of shit. Good for the cheeky, slimy fuckers. Otufa would chase away the rats and begin to work at forcing the excrement down the drains with his hands without twitching his nose. He would then wash his hands thoroughly when he had finished with a harsh detergent. The highlights of his life and his fellow workers were when Olu Ray occasionally gave his hand for them to shake. They treasured such moments because they believed that someone at least had not forgotten their humanity, that someone was bold enough to shake the hands that forced shit down the drains each and everyday. Sometimes, one of them would hold out their hand for Olu to shake for that precious, life-giving acknowledgement. At such moments, he flinched but still received the handshake. The men began to put even more trust in him. The surprising thing was that they never asked him for money and he never offered them any. He felt money would defy the spiritual sanctity of their bond. People shunned them and they on their part did not go out of their way to ingratiate themselves. They possessed the most exquisite manners in spite of having very little formal education. Olu would sometimes make them presents of parcels of foods which they received gladly. There was nothing corrupting about food. He also used to tell them that he would give out mountains of food when he had enough money and they would smile telling him not to make promises he could not keep. He would reply that he truly meant what he had said. Before he left the town to go on national service, he began to notice some signs of physical deterioration in the Bulldozer. In the past, Otufa had a brusque, energetic gait that later became gauche, forced and donkey-like. His original gait had a good measure of fluidity and it was a pain to see pushing him on, trying to fill every moment of his existence with his past indefatigable energy. Olu would ask him if his powers had left him but the Bulldozer would always reply in the negative no matter how run-down his condition was; he could never give in, it never even seemed to occur to him. Olu sometimes sat on some object by the roadside to watch his secret teacher carrying his rusty battered bucket from pump to shithole and he knew the man's powers were slowly but surely seeping away with a persistence that moved like the implacable hand of death. But no, the Bulldozer would never give in, he would never admit his most hidden and most persistent fear. He would also persist in affirming his endurance, his strength, with the same shamanic stoicism. Olu would smile or even laugh softly, but the iridescence in his laughter was no longer warm and deep. It was a hallow laugh to maintain good manners. From then on, a lighted stream of sorrow became more dominant than Olu's laughter. Olu did not mention this to him, there was no point in attempting to soften the steel-encrusted soul of a man who had made up his mind to die standing with his eyes widened to the sun. He was a man who could only die with his tattered slippers on. Olu could sometimes feel that the Bulldozer's being had been racked with so much hardship and suffering that better conditions would be too strange to him. Everyday, hardship and suffering tussled to settle scores on his slowly collapsing body. His body had become the ground on which they pursued their diurnal rages. And every night, they made him sleep with them, made him abide by them with or without his will. He seemed to have no choice in the matter even though he was equally relentless.

A colleague of Otufa's became the victim of ineffable hardship and suffering. He was called Loco Tade. He was of medium height and he had a great big stomach which seemed to be always rumbling. He called the perennial rumbling in his belly the drumming of the worms of dusk. He hardly spoke to any one and no one spoke to him either except in necessary circumstances. His work clothes were always filthy and he wore them at most times. He walked as if he had entire planets bogging him down, smoking his cheap foul-smelling cigarettes. People whispered that he had been afflicted by plagues but no one knew for sure the nature of these plagues. Around his large red eyes, little white worms emerged which he wiped away with his shirt sleeves at irregular intervals. If he suddenly stopped dead, not many people would have noticed because it was a wonder how he had managed to stay alive for so long. He would appear in the doorways of eating places and people would vacate the joint for good never to come back. He was bad luck and bad business for such places. The reek of death had remained so long with him that it had grown stale. It was this condition that Olu feared Otufa would eventually lapse into; a deathlike purgatory filled with the most dreary vapours and endless gloom. For Otufa, it seemed to be just the beginning. A fresh putrescent odour began to ooze out of his body signifying the entry of final decay. Olu would wonder if he would recover fully from an illness that may completely eat up his body. Olu hoped that Otufa would not end up like Loco Tade with worms coming out his eyes and orifices. Now the best men in the world for whom Otufa the Bulldozer was a chief priest had rolled dream-bearing gales into the night to meet Olu to remind him of his promises and the need to return.

46

When it was dawn, he had whitish marks left by tears on his cheeks. He hadn't shed any tears of sentimentality, he had shed those tears out of the stoniness of his heart. They didn't mean a damn because as the cold tears dripped he had the cold breath of death seething in his belly. Of course, it is easy to say fuck sentimentality. As usual, his friend Hugo, lay sleeping and looked unperturbed. But Hugo was disturbed when the people around him started to engage in early morning activities; morning devotion, the washing of mosquito-bitten faces, the brushing of teeth, the shake-down of crumpled clothes and the like. One had to hit the road either in search of idleness or work. It didn't matter because sometimes even idleness is hard to come by. Soon the doors of the offices were open to the public and some of the noble servants went in to have a more thorough wash or use the toilets. As this was going on, Hugo and Olu did the usual cleaning. Whilst doing that, they got attracted by two women who did not appear to be born-again Christians or gold-diggers at a time when girls had to belong to one of the camps. The men drew them into conversation and they seemed pleasant enough. They even agreed to meet with them later in the day. Both friends congratulated themselves on finally hitting bull's-eye. Their days of drought seemed to be coming to an end. In joy, they decided to go for a well-deserved shit in a nearby wood. Hugo for one, felt like baring his ebony arse to the rising rays of the sun. He preferred to shit in the open with spiky ends of blades of grass pricking him in the bum. He loved to feel the wind spiking his bottom with fine grains of sand. He thought it was one of the most beautiful sensations in existence (after fucking of course). Olu, on his part, was not especially keen on such bare-arsed indecency and pleasures. He felt it was rather demeaning when viewed from a rather hoity-toity, upturned-nose perspective. He was particularly afraid of snakes because it was common to find them lodged beneath the grass and undergrowth waiting for prey or simply chilling out. The sun

47

was still behind them and Hugo backed it to catch its early morning warmth. He was not very far from the roadside and it was possible for him to be seen by pedestrians but what did he care? Having a crap equals having a crap. Full stop. Besides no one knew him in the town. He even winked at some passersby who took more than a passing interest in him. All seemed to be going well until the two young women whom they had chatted up earlier approached them. Olu was the first to see them and by then it was too late to run away or hide. The women were shocked beyond words to find their new acquaintances shitting in public. They hadn't appeared to be the kind of men who would shit or fuck in public. The women were vain, conventional and plain and did not expect anything out of the ordinary. They had been looking forward to seeing the men again. The vainer of the two launched into a long tirade about the need for a strict code of behaviour to regulate the wilder impulses of the general populace. She went on holding and twitching her nose and sometimes even spat on the ground to show her disgust. The two men were too confounded to even pull up their pants and remained squatting on their haunches with their exposed buttocks and dangling dicks. Their pendulous dicks made them look like criminals on a short vacation. They seemed like two convicts that had broken ranks with a chain-gang. Vanity got the better of the woman and as to be expected she overdid things. It dawned on Hugo that all was lost and that it was no use aspiring to a boring sense of public decency. An animal caught out in its natural habitat ought to be nothing but an animal. It ought to eat, shit, fuck and kill like an animal. And so Hugo barked at her to back the fuck off before he peed on her. She uttered a few more rude words but she and her astonished friend backed away. Both men felt their slight emotional discomfort ease and they pulled up their pants. It was better not to think too much about what had happened. Sure some people would make fun of them but it would all soon be forgotten. Olu cared about

48

what people would think but Hugo simply couldn't give a fuck. Hugo had once been a village urchin and he and his mates shat on garbage dumps and in the woods all through their pre-teen years. So shitting in public wasn't new to him. He felt it was cool to shit on the vestibule of the palace of good manners without giving two fucks about hypocritical decency. He believed being able to do this was cooler than the final acid trip into mental nirvana.

But for Olu even though it was something he did from time to time, it was also something that brought him a fair amount of shame.

Why don't you let's go and beg them not to tell anyone...I mean ask for their forgiveness ? Asked Olu as they went along.

Forget about those bitches. I'll just tell them they had better keep their big mouths shut otherwise I'll slit their throats.

Those words put a little courage into Olu who was really worried about what would become of his reputation. Not that he had much of a reputation actually but at least he possessed a degree of anonymity which suited him. He had for instance, not killed anyone or committed any great offence. He went about his business taking care not to wrong anybody or allowing himself to be wronged. In this sense, he was a suspect character since he would not lead nor allow himself to be led. And now he might gain notoriety as a defiler of public morality and places. A common and scandalous noontime bottom displayer. A lowlife flasher. An offender of finer sensibilities. A participant in crappy visuals. He could not understand why his friend did not feel the same way. How could he afford to be so unconcerned with fears regarding a besmirched reputation?

When they got back to the offices, Olu felt as if all eyes were trained upon him. He had a phobia that every ear had heard about the act they had committed. His friend just couldn't be bothered. He went about instead with a supercilious frown on his face; a serious young man who had very pressing matters to which to attend. On that day, they both decided that they were going to leave the place they had made their abode. Those few nights of sleeping outside had the effect of robbing them of good sense and basic decency. They resolved to humanise themselves by attaining a measure of good life, by looking for old fashioned virtues like habitable housing and fresh beddings. Both men had been assigned to work in different establishments but they had not showed up at them. This was because it had taken so much trouble to get posted to those places in the first instance. All things, as they say, depended on having some dough. One almost had to pay for the air one consumed. A bunch of opportunistic despots might shoot their way into power and carry out some diabolical Fourieristic and Darwinian designs to decimate an unchecked population. Many destitutes could sometimes be heard murmuring to themselves thanking God for their lives of beggary.

So as was the norm, the two friends had had to bribe the officials in charge of the postings. A man was always tempted to do that since the lousy officials invariably preferred to sleep with women who paid their dues in that manner. For a man, cash was it and that was the end of the matter. Homosexuals were closeted. No one knew what happened to them in the shadows they haunted. No one bothered to scrutinise their bipolar existence. They had chosen a life of concealment. They had nurtured a love that must remain nameless. But within those fathomless shadows, people were getting fucked up the arse.

Hugo went to his place of work and Olu followed suit after agreeing to meet again as soon as they had both settled. Olu felt particularly glad about having been posted to a state-owned bank. First of all, he should to be comfortably accommodated and paid generous amounts for his upkeep. Secondly, a lot of his colleagues had been posted there so he was certain to find good company. When he got to the bank, he was welcomed and a driver was assigned to take him to where he was to be domiciled. Olu got there and saw that it was a comfortable affair. The floors were carpeted (albeit soiled) and an air-conditioner worked even if it grumbled loudly. One other man had already been living there. Olu got one of the still available bedrooms and slumped upon a large bed. He scanned the walls which were not so dusty. He had a fairly good table, a fragile plastic chair and also an old but decent arm-chair. Two electric bulbs in the room were functional and he had a whole wardrobe to himself even if its door had been removed from its hinges. Counting his small mercies, he laid back and fell into a deep sleep with his shoes on. The nights of sleeping outside exposed to the chill and mosquitoes at the bureau had completely worn him out. It wasn't noon yet when he fell asleep and he did not wake up until late evening after one of his flat mates knocked persistently on the door to find out if all was well. His name was Friday and Olu came to know in time that he was a pleasant chap. The following day, two other guys arrived and all the rooms in the flat became occupied.

For two weeks, they lived together like one small happy family. They took turns in going to the market to shop for one another and took turns in cooking. Even the dishes where washed in turns. It was a fine little flat that sparkled with jokes and laughter. After the first two weeks, things began to turn sour when a girl brought a letter 'from above' permitting her to eject one of the new occupants. Every one was stunned but no one said a word. An aqueduct of bad blood had been laid in the flat. Bad blood meant evil feeling and dark clouded bellies. The occupant had to move into the sitting-room and his other flat mates offered to harbour his gear. Bad blood stifled the laughter of the flat. The guys no longer laughed as freely and openly as before. Angelina who had caused bad blood would bring all manner of middle-aged alhajis to the flat and take over the living room with her irreverence. She looked down on the guys and would attempt to make them feel inferior by boasting about her lavish spending sprees and the wealth of her numerous boyfriends. Each night, she brought in at least two bottles of wine or champagne in a town where alcohol was supposed to be forbidden. Where she got them from, no one knew. She brought a few friends along and together they would deride the alhajis who lavished so much money on her. Another girl Lolly, brought another letter 'from above' instructing the other new occupant of the flat to move out for her. He too moved into the sitting room and by then a dam of bad blood had burst in the flat. Life became horrid for those two unfortunate men as they had to wait for girls' visitors to leave late at night before they could sleep. Their sleeping hours were cut short and levels of irritability mounted. When they complained to the two girls, they replied that the sitting room was for everybody. The men slept on cushions laid on the floor and now they had to beg to get some sleep. It was getting simply unbearable.

Matters came to a head when two more girls brought high-powered letters from above authorising Olu and Friday to vacate their rooms. Friday started to complain that if he were to come back into the world again, he would come back as a woman. He pondered the possibilities of becoming a Koran-toting transvestite. He didn't feel he could endure the agony of a life destined for the shadows. Men would pour scorn on him during the daytime and the same men would return at night with faces hidden underneath turbans to fuck him at night. During the day, women and children would mock and insult him with songs as he passed. The sun would reject him. Dark shadows would tremble as he approached. To Friday, women seemed to be receiving the best things in life when they were not locked away in religious seclusion. It was just a matter of sleeping with the right man in the right place. Constance was the name of the well-connected girl who took over his room. She wasn't pretty at all and she wore loads of make-up. She had a little tribal scar on each cheek and she was the notice-me-or-I'll-die type. Her ultimate aim in life was to make men drool and she had a number of ways of doing so. For instance, she was famous for her sitting positions by which she displayed her upper thighs and panties. She had lovely inner thighs to go with a venomous tongue. She had long bleached hair, an over-sized derriere and she had a small unsexy waist. That was Constance for you, she could be as enticing as an edenic seductress and those suspect charms of hers carried the seeds of male destruction. Friday discovered this soon enough. Everyone agreed that it would be an eye-sore if the dispossessed men were to keep their stuff in the living room so they decided to leave them in their former rooms until such time a better arrangement emerged. But this temporary state of affairs did not suit girls like Constance. They wanted the boys out of the rooms effectively and if possible out of the entire flat. Constance wanted all vestiges of Friday out of her newly-acquired room immediately and she was not ready to compromise on this point. Friday pleaded with her to no avail. Then she carried the disagreement to another level. She would go out for hours or even days end, locking her door and not leaving her key behind so the poor guy could not have access to his stuff. He would be reduced to borrowing shirts and other personal effects and sometimes he even had to miss going to work. He implored her again and again to at least try to be a little more considerate but she would only throw her nose up in the air. Out, she said, out of my life with you! She even told him that she disappeared for days on end because she could not stand the sight of his face. She would scream at him that he was wearing her nerves thin. On many occasions, she threatened to hit him across the face and the poor guy would attempt to placate her in the best way he knew. Usually the situation only grew worse. Then one day, during one of their arguments, she got beside herself with anger and slapped Friday on the face. He was too stunned to respond in a similar manner but dared her to do it again. She didn't wait for the challenge to lapse when she struck again with even greater force. The violence attracted those who were in the flat to the scene. The guys- who were mainly chauvinists- would have felt disgraced if quarrelsome Constance had gotten away scot-free with two hot slaps. Friday threw her a blow and she landed on her buttocks. She emitted a gut-wrenching wail. Commotion broke loose. Angelina and Lolly who were around and had been waiting to see a melee, helped Constance back onto her feet, urging her all the while not to take the blow lying low. They both hissed at Friday and called him a brute as Constance continued to wail that she had been maimed. Everyone thought the matter would end there until she went into the kitchen and picked a knife which she hid behind her back. She stabbed Friday on the back. It was Friday's turn to cry.

The matter was taken up at the official levels and at the end of it all both Constance and Friday were dismissed and the remaining occupants in the flat were ordered to move out to avoid a recurrence of similar incidents.

*****

Olu Ray was fortunate to find a room through the influence of a well-connected man who worked at his bank. It was a splendid room by the standards of the town. He had his own toilet and bath and a large comfortable bed. It was leagues better than any hole he had been expecting to get. It even had an old poster with semi-nude blondes on the wall. He thought about throwing a party but he eventually dropped the idea. Surprisingly, the taps in the bathroom worked but there was a strong musty smell. He needed some air - freshener to try and solve the small problem. He ought to have been screaming from joy. He hoped that he would be allowed to stay in the room for as long as was necessary and not be forced out like the other time. He had a bath and read some magazines lying on the bed.

The following morning, he took his bath and went to work. After work, he came back to his room feeling quite exhausted. After a few weeks, he began to invite some friends to his room and they told him he was lucky to be living like a monarch. He knew he was lucky when he compared his lot with his colleagues who had to sleep in rooms with broken beds or furniture. He couldn't help it if he was fortunate. Some of his friends slept in rooms that had no fans to reduce the heat or window-panes to keep out the chill and mosquitoes at night. Many of them begged him to allow them to stay with him but he told them they could only come by on weekends. He wanted to maintain an amount of privacy to be able to pursue his thoughts as freely as he wished. After a while, he sometimes felt living alone was not such a good idea. He would come back from work to confront complete solitude and silence. At night, the winds would rap on the window-panes and the door would squeak from the flow of the draught. There would be no human sounds nearby to keep him company. The highlight of his evening was the preparation of his meal. He wasn't a fantastic cook but he knew one or two gastronomic sleights he could perform with eggs, onions and tomatoes. He would brew himself a kettle of strong tea after his meal and then went back to lie on his empty bed, browsing over and over again, the same old magazines. Two months of adhering to the same routines almost drove him up the wall. A few times, during weekends, he had invited friends over to come and spend some time with him. His loneliness was more piercing when they left. What he needed, he thought, was a girl. He did not need her to do chores for him. He only needed her for his bed. He wished for a partner who would not be an emotional and financial drain on him. But he in turn did not have much to give except to provide her with a few basic comforts. And where was one to find such a partner in a sexually segregated town? This was a town that kept women behind closed doors all their lives; where they were taught not to look at men too directly in the eye; where they wore veils and long arabesque gowns that made unimaginative attempts to arrest the imagination. None of these measures were successful in terms of maintaining strict puritanical mores. Underneath all the heavy dark flowing gowns and social manners, a hectic undercurrent of sexual deviancy was always at play.

Along with some friends, Olu Ray began to discover more about the town. At night, they prowled about looking for the drinking bars that had prostitutes and where marijuana was smoked. Eventually, they avoided dens that sold grass but stuck instead to bars that sold hard liquor and beer. The bars at nightfall looked like places for illicit sex and not just harmless revelry. They reeked of ancient sex, liquor and armpits.

Sex-workers were usually in most of the bars. They were the only females one saw in social situations that involved merry-making. Their mode of dress was no different from married women who lived in purdah; veils and plain long gowns over slippers or sandals.

Alhajis would be seen cruising around secluded brothels with little bottles of gin in their pockets looking for a night of quick, hidden unIslamic sex. Wads of cash would be falling out of their bulging pockets onto the bosoms of free women. In these matters, it was a town in which night never met with day. The two were kept separate by a gingerly placed hypocritical smile.

One night, Olu went out for drinks with two friends and as usual, there were hookers loitering around. Olu hadn't much money so he decided to concentrate on his beer. Nonetheless, he could not avoid noticing a particularly pretty woman. She kept moving in and out of the inner rooms at intervals. Shortly afterwards, having finished a couple of beers, Hassan, one of Olu's friends went off with her and did not turn up until two hours later. She wasn't tall and she had a fair complexion. Her eyes had a cool and an almost aristocratic detachment in them. She wore a long black dress that had shining silver stones on it. She also wore a dark shawl over a head. It was impossible to learn from Hassan how good she was in bed because he was a cynical fellow who never told the truth about his sex life.

Ali, Olu's other companion who had a warmer and more forthright personality, had also taken a young woman into one of the inner rooms and when he came out he was full of complaints. Hassan kept trying to shut Ali up. His grouse was that the girl had been in the middle of her period. She had sold sex to a man earlier before him and had stained the sheets with fresh blood. He didn't notice the stains until they had finished. In anger, he called her a devil. She gave him the evil eye but did not utter a word. Those girls would do anything for money, he claimed. Olu listened with keen interest as they walked home in freezing temperatures. But those sexual distractions were not frequent. At night, Olu would stay awake fantasising about harems filled with oriental virgins, public baths set in acres of marble, Turkish paradises and martyrdom, and death by sex. He pondered the gulf between his imagination and reality as well as the uses of schizophrenia as a means of redressing the flaws of capitalism. All this did not change the fact he needed a woman.

He struck up a friendship with Oskar Jekker, a brilliant young scholar who worked with the state-owned newspaper. Because Oskar had a brilliant mind Olu who often visited him where he lived along with other colleagues in the quarters the newspaper had provided them. In those quarters, that had many rooms, there lived a woman called Stephanie Machi. Stephanie wasn't particularly beautiful but she had a gorgeous physique. She was also aware of her gifts and how to make good use of them. She had long well-shaped legs which she showed off frequently. Apart from these endowments, she hadn't much going for her. She had a shallow mind that possessed little powers of concentration. To her, it wasn't such a bad idea coming to the edge of the desert. She had been told that there were many wealthy men who were always looking for women on whom to spend their money. It didn't matter that most of these men were middle-aged and overweight or that they sometimes stank. The long and short of it was that she had decided not to go out with the guys of her own age because they could not provide her with her material needs. She thought this was the best decision she had ever made in her life.

Stephanie did really have a fine pair of legs and a lovely behind. Oskar, who was reading a tome that had not been approved by the Islamic Board of Censors, in other words, an illicit volume, had began a scholarly treatise of which Stephanie was the sole subject. It was called "Towards a Phenomenology of the Buttocks" which was meant to be a neo-Hegelian anti-metaphysical construct deliberating on open-ended, post-human dimensions of sex. He spent time perusing the world's erotic classics to provide him with enough inspiration for his project. But Stephanie herself provided him with sufficient erotic impetus when she displayed her muse-generating thighs around the complex of rooms wearing a skimpy pair of shorts. She certainly gave off a degree of charm as she went from room to room hurling dognose-sized chunks of meat at her neighbours. She, in her mind, was simply a star. The rest of the girls who lived in the complex did not possess her tempting attributes and contented themselves with modest roles. As usual, there were two camps; those who approved of commercial sex work and those who preferred to stick with the Lord. In spite of the divisions within the scene, Stephanie was still queen. Olu Ray got friendly with her and she promised to introduce him to some alhajis she knew who wanted English tutors for their wives and daughters. Olu could not wait to begin. But Stephanie was such a forgetful person and he had to frequently remind her about her promise. However, soon enough she was to make good her word.

One night, a curious incident happened in Stephanie's complex. She stayed in the best room in the compound which was stocked with an assortment of expensive electronic gadgets and household equipment donated by her numerous alhaji paramours. She had a small oriental sofa upon which she could act out the role of an odalisque or a belly dancer for her generous benefactors. One night, she was reclining on the sofa with her head upon David's thighs, her boyfriend who was gently smoothening her hair. Earlier in the day, frolicsome and forgetful Stephanie invited twelve of her alhaji boyfriends to take her out separately. She did it as a joke but it went on to have huge reverberations. Oskar sat in the long, empty passage of the complex reading an illicit erotic volume when the alhajis began to arrive. A few of the educated ones among the visitors saw that he was reading sacrilegious material but remained silent.

Stephanie had pushed David away into the room of one her colleagues while she entertained her rich pot-bellied friends. When the twelve of them had managed to squeeze themselves into her little room, each one of them believed they would be the lucky one to win the chance of spending the night with Stephanie. Stephanie, of course, got busy serving drinks to her boyfriends and even giving some of them kisses until she became quite flustered. All of them had brought gifts along with them which they took turns in presenting to her. Her bed was soon littered with presents. She didn't even bother to open many of them. Conversation was a two-way affair and not generalised as the alhajis avoided speaking to one another. Instead, they concentrated their efforts on winning the attention of Stephanie. A bold man called out Stephanie to discuss the issue of her spending the night with him and Stephanie took him to the room of one of her colleagues to settle the matter. However, she did not settle it before she rushed back to meet her other guests. One by one, the other alhajis came out trying to strike a deal with Stephanie. She, in turn, led them to the rooms of her various colleagues. When some of her guests realised that it was impossible to take her away for the night they started suggesting sleeping with her in the rooms she had put them.

Stephanie did nothing to discourage those suggestions and may indeed have encouraged them because some the alhajis undressed, shivering in the cold waiting for her. It was incredible- twelve well-established men, shivering and waiting for a quick dampener for their desires at a complex located in a slum. Stephanie spent the entire night running from room to room placating and assuring the naked men. At the first crow of the cock, many of them started to believe that she wasn't giving out herself or sharing her desires and began to get dressed in order to return to their homes and perhaps comfort their abused wives. They trudged to their luxurious vehicles swearing and at the same time proclaiming the greatness of Allah.

However, one alhaji insisted on sleeping with Stephanie who gave him a cutting look saying, but alhaji you've only got one testicle, how could you possibly sleep with me now when those that have two have not? And true enough the man had only one large testicle which hung like a ball. He looked about him stealthily and only laughed when he saw no one was around.

When they had all gone, Stephanie did not bother to go and comfort her boyfriend who had travelled from afar to see her. Instead, she slept in a separate room with a girlfriend. The following day was Friday and all the twelve unfortunate alhajis met at the central mosque after the jumat service and swore collectively to chase all infidels out of town.

And Stephanie, the architect of the entire comedy of errors left David, her bona fide boyfriend alone in the complex and went away without telling him to laugh over the previous night's joke with some friends who lived some way off. David had nothing to eat because Stephanie preferred to eat out and hardly cooked. He was reduced to accepting hand-outs from some of Stephanie's neighbours. When she finally came back she remained unapologetic believing she could deploy her feminine charms to solve any problem. Friends of hers who intended to adopt her lifestyle came to seek advice. Shortly afterwards, David prepared to return to his home but he told a few people in the complex that it was over between him and Stephanie. He promised to seek vengeance over how he had been abused.

Oskar hadn't progressed much with his project on female eroticism and spent much of his time browsing through the offensive pages of proscribed tomes. He read in the long empty passage, waiting and hoping to get good displays of Stephanie's legs when she came out of her room. He hadn't thought much about disclosing his project to his principal subject, experience had told him that she would denigrate and abuse it. Secondly, he wanted the work to be of real scholarly interest and such matters were certain to bore Stephanie and might even annoy her. In between time spent reading offensive volumes, he devoted his energies to writing a piece on sexual puns again employing Stephanie as a primary source of inspiration. What he did not know though, was that a few alhajis had observed him reading illicit texts.

Soon afterwards, Stephanie's coterie of female followers began to grow daily. The group met everyday to compare notes about how to deal with men. Stephanie was nicknamed the stockbroker since she bought and sold the desires of men. As her trade boomed, so did her detractors. Her room came to be known as the Borehole and rumours of orgies concerning what transpired there spread. Stephanie blithely ignored the mutterings. Amaka, one of her converts had biting wit. She would ridicule the alhajis for their unromantic chat-up lines and her favourite joke was about the manner in which a man would seek to attract a hot-looking chick.

He would stop his sleek car beside you as you stood waiting for a taxi, she would begin, and then he would take a look at you as one does when one wants to buy a cow or a goat. If he felt you weren't good enough, he would drive off to scan other places in town until he found a girl of his choice. But if he fancied you, he would invite you into his ride and of course you would be obliged to enter. He would begin by saying something about lunch and wouldn't even seek your opinion, it was as if you had no choice and you were a starving victim. He would drive to one of the better hotels in town and order for you, everything on the menu. I mean everything, such vulgar philanthropists. So you might have chicken, beef and fish dishes all before you, a wide assortment of soups, potatoes, yam, egg, plantain, fried rice, jollof, plain rice, everything, the works. Pork was the only thing not in front of you. And while you were trying to concentrate on the few dishes that caught your eye, he would have paid for a room to fuck you in. Such lousy bastards. I mean he thinks because he had bought you meal he has the right to rip off your panties. Whilst you were eating, he never said a word to you and sat smoking cigarettes as his life depended on them. I mean smoke would be coming out of his nose, ears and off the top of his head. You finished eating what you were able to and he'd urge you fervently to eat more, I mean, literally try to force down the entire arsenal down your fucking throat. It didn't matter to him that he had disgraced you by treating you like a glutton in the first place in his bid to make you a spineless geisha. When you refused his aggressive hospitality, and stood up to go saying thanks, he would shove you into a corridor saying he wanted a chat with you. Throughout the meal, it never occurred to him to seize the opportunity but of course out of politeness you followed him and he continued bungling until he had taken you into a dimly lit room. It was then you knew what he was up to. He wouldn't say a word to you, he would just begin to remove his robes and trousers until you told him, alright stop I'm getting out of here. You had to be strong on this point because it is your persistence that would make him leave you alone. He isn't very keen on creating a scandal because of course he is known all about town. Finally, he would storm off in annoyance leaving you behind or he becomes as meek as a lamb when you told him you weren't that sort of girl and then he drives you to your destination never to bother you again and assuring you to call on him if you needed any help. Here's a piece of advice, those are the sort of men you should pursue. You can easily milk them dry without their knowing for nothing.

Amaka was next to Stephanie as a figure of authority until something strange happened to her. She disappeared for about two weeks and when she came back she was looking ill and emaciated. Something terrible had happened to her because she had aged, her long hair was falling off, the hair on her brows was gone, her gums had a sickly colour and her breath smelled bad. She began her story: Many nights ago I was waiting as usual to be picked up by a man when this tall handsome Adonis stopped by me. I mean he was really gorgeous and I was hoping he wasn't married. He took me to an expensive restaurant to have the usual meal but instead of taking me to a classy hotel to fuck, he took me to this cheap seedy brothel in a secluded part of town. I wasn't too worried because I thought he was only a stickler for privacy and I had made up my mind that I wanted him. The other thing about this man was that he had such suave manners, I mean like a prince. I didn't even wait for him to ask me to take off my clothes before I took them off myself. But he was so proper about everything, I mean he really took his time and smiled charmingly as he walked around the room placing his gold wristwatch carefully on the table and uttering sweet nothings to me. My body ached with impatience for him to come to the bed. The room had a single green bulb and had an awful smell like any other cheap brothel room. But I didn't mind; I wanted to be with my catch. I shut my eyes and waited for him. When he finally did he was so big that he had to push and push causing me some pain but I lay almost motionless so that we could become one. And when he fully entered me, I couldn't feel his body - I thought it was unusual that he kept

63

thrusting without touching me. At last, I held out my arms to reach him but they merely groped in the dark. So I opened my eyes and saw a greenish serpent going in and out of me, I screamed only to pass out. Ngozi, one of the prostitutes who lived in the brothel came to my rescue and became my saviour. She claimed not to have seen the serpent, but saw a box of cardboard filled with money at the end of the bed. When I came to, I was treated by traditional means because people said my case was beyond the understanding of western medical science. The healers performed a lot of sacrifices on my behalf but they say I will never be fully well again and that they could only prolong my life for a while. I am telling you all this so that the world would know about my fate and so that I would not pass away in vain. I saying this to you because it could happen to you and I want you to be careful. You can't miss this guy. He's devilishly handsome and I'm sure he would strike again. We have to plan how to catch him in the act. We have to stop him before he ruins more lives. We all have to stand together to fight this new virus. Divided we fall together we stand.

Before Amaka ended her story, the hearts of all the girls around all but stopped beating. Many whispered when they had collected themselves that they would rather have the worse kind of virus than have a serpent go into them. A few faint-hearted ones amongst them said it was the end of their sexual dealings with men. The woeful story spread about town but the defiant Stephanie could not be bothered. Amaka could go to hell as far as she was concerned and she was determined to go on plying her trade, serpent or no serpent. However her reputation slipped from being a kept woman to being a common whore. But as usual, it was no great matter to her. A few months later, Amaka died after her plight had been narrated before millions of television viewers. Before then, rumours had become rampant about men who made love to women in serpentine form to make money. It was a practice *juju* and *muti* practitioners knew so well.

However, the spread of such fears did not diminish the need for sex. Not even death could.

Amaka's death caused a considerable amount of controversy in the town. To begin with, the mysterious circumstances surrounding her demise affected tourism and the image of the town. So the government was particularly anxious to cast the affair into oblivion but it was clear that it made some grievous mistakes in its attempt. First of all, the governor once again proscribed all texts that had not received the approval of the Islamic Censors Board. The proscription was in fact the work of the culture commissioner who held the belief that such works were capable of turning one's mind upside down. In the university, students made huge bonfires, destroying all alleged mind-bending literatures. Needless to say, Oskar was flabbergasted by the pervasive orgy of destruction and hid away his beloved texts on eroticism and necrophilia. There was a dogged but clumsy attempt to blot out the memory of Amaka but her death hung over the town like an implacable silhouette. Instead of honouring the dead woman's memory with a respectable modicum of silence, street urchins took over the town with catapults raiding all known brothels because it was believed that whores were responsible for the town's woes. The urchins not only shot at girls who lived in brothels, some of the more hardened ones raped them. Many churches were burnt that had worshipping Christians in them. Hundreds of Christians and innocent pedestrians lost their lives. Infidels were hunted down in broad daylight and stoned to death. Stores owned by the non-religious were burnt to the ground. Urchins rampaged for days in an orgy of looting and lawlessness. Soldiers were not left out in the quest for blood and they too participated in the rapes and looting. Several prostitutes who had been killed after being brutally gang-raped were burnt and their charred remains were left lying on the bloodied streets to be eaten by stray dogs.

The rioting was unprecedented and what the authorities feared most had happened, the image of the town became irreversibly tarnished. Suddenly, the government developed a phobia for journalists. At first, it debated the merits of killing all brilliant investigative journalists with parcel bombs but the culture commissioner put in a strong word against such fascist scheme. The public outcry to such a plan would be more than the power-brokers would be able to contain. Then a more ingenious measure was put forward. All snooping journalists were to be bribed using means as diverse as raw cash, women, drugs or booze failing which they were to be dispatched in staged car accidents. Many of them fell for the bribes. There was a sad case about a greedy journalist who wanted three conditions; cash, women and booze. What made it even more pathetic was the fact that he had a wife and family. For three months, he was comfortably accommodated in a government rest house where he passed through a period of intense dissolution. Everyday three girls were brought to him, three different girls that is, each day and after some time there was no need to put on his clothes because there was always some action going on. The booze flowed constantly until he succumbed to a permanent alcoholic haze. At home, his wife had been thinking some harm had come to him until she discovered him falling apart under the weight of booze and women. She almost cried her eyes out and the sad part was that her husband hardly knew what was happening, he had sunken so deeply into his corruption. She put his trousers on for him and led him shirtless to the airport homeward bound. It would take him a few years to put back together again the broken pieces of his life, marriage and career. He was lucky that he had a tolerant and understanding wife.

In the long run only a few consciences kept alive the memory of Amaka's death. Written accounts which would have been ideal for that purpose had all been destroyed with the complicity of librarians and journalists. There was no national or international outpouring over the rapes and looting, there was no categorical condemnation of the widespread carnage, and there was no memorial to the dead. And with the implacable calm after a desert storm, the activities of the town commenced again with the usual slow burning pace.

*****

One night, Stephanie was out as usual to play the street tart. The weather was not cold as it could be and she had on a vermillion mini-dress that displayed her legs. She felt like heaven holding her small white handbag and backing a line of shops that had closed for the day. The street was pretty deserted but there was no danger nearby. The good thing about the town was that one could hang out till anytime and street girls were free to haunt the dark alleys as daringly as they wished. Stephanie felt energetic in the warm night as she held out her face to occasional drifting breezes to inhale some freshness. Her lucky star shone upon her when a handsome stallion-like automobile pulled up beside her. On that night, Stephanie was not feeling arrogant -in fact she was filled with considerable goodwill, she was flowing with considerable faith. She walked sensually to the stationary car and leaned against one of its doors with an easy feline grace to see who was inside. Stephanie's good spirits held out. She entered the car and the man drove off. Apart from saying hello, how are you, he said nothing else and Stephanie did not bother to disturb him with needless conversation. Slowly, they made their way towards a brothel located in the central part of town. The man paid for a room and they both went inside. Used condoms and bits and pieces of used tissue paper were strewn about the floor but the bed had been freshly laid. The man got upon the bed and asked Stephanie to sit upon him and tickle him. She did as she was told and the man gave some stifled unhealthy laughs until he suddenly stopped. At first, Stephanie thought it was all a joke and continued to tickle and taunt the motionless man until it became apparent that he was dead. She almost gave a loud scream but she checked herself, adjusted her clothes, and sneaked as quietly as possible out of the brothel and eventually came upon the street. She ran heedlessly into the night until she was fortunate to pick up a taxi that conveyed her home. When she got home, she did not mention a word about the tragedy to anyone. But she made a vow to herself - she decided to go steady with one man from then onwards.

Two days later, the death of the man made newspaper headlines. He was a prominent businessman called Alhaji Isa Umar. He had six wives and thirty-two children. Of course, the papers did not mention where his dead body had been found but it was stated that he died of a heart attack. Buried in a hole, underneath his ancient bed were three steel boxes filled with dollars. But during his lifetime, the dead man had been so mean-fisted his family went for entire weeks without meat or fish. His numerous children went about looking haggard and beggarly. They were no different from the street urchins who fought over leftovers at roadside shacks. His death though was a blow to the whole community because he had been a paragon of sheer industry, thrift and religious diligence.

Stephanie had never been so frightened in her life. A beacon of the community had died right beneath her and there was a possibility that an elaborate inquiry might be conducted using both orthodox and unorthodox means. At night, she would cling tightly to her pillow for succour. She spent sleepless nights biting her lips until dawn. Two weeks passed and no policemen or secret agents came knocking at her door and then she began to sleep more easily once again. Nonetheless, she still promised herself to stick to her vow.

A few men came her way but she wasn't besotted with any of them until a colonel, Ahmed Zorro, who was a brigade commander came into her life. He was a pudgy, ugly man with large tribal scars who already had two wives at home. From the beginning, he made it clear to Stephanie that he wanted to keep her as his paramount mistress. Stephanie wasn't apprehensive about his proposal because it was something she had sought. The conditions were that he would accommodate her in a splendidly fitted guest house, complete with television sets, DVD players and the latest hi-fi systems. She would also be provided with enough money to buy all the clothes she wanted. But she was not, upon the pain of death, to bring any man into her residence. Neither could she keep any boyfriends outside her abode. The conditions were acceptable to Stephanie. A few days later an army truck was brought to her place to convey her things to the guest house where she was now to stay. The white bungalow was a high society girl's dream. She even had a steward attached to her. She had to do nothing but shop. The chauffeur would take her to the main shopping arcade where she bought everything that caught her fancy until she became bored. She became a perfect example of crass postcolonial consumerism. By that time, she had enough clothes in her closets to last her at least two whole years.

At home, she had an extensive DVD and video library to keep her mind occupied. In the refrigerators, were edibles of an astonishing range. All day long, she put her feet upon a couple of oriental cushions and watched films. At evenings, her man would come and unwind by her side. Most times, he would have a meal and then retire to bed with her for a couple of hours and when it struck eleven o 'clock he returned home to his family. This was the turn Stephanie's life more or less took. She could not go out unless escorted by a soldier. There was a permanent soldier stationed at the gate of the guest house. He was a lance corporal of about forty-five years of age named Solomon. A short while afterwards, Stephanie became thoroughly bored with her existence. She even began to find the incredible opulence that surrounded her disgusting. She longed for the thrills and risks of her former life. And then an idea struck her. She could get friendly with Solomon and then she would be able to have her way with him. She only had to wait until a favourable opportunity turned up.

There had been a great deal of bitterness in Solomon's life. As a child, he had been orphaned and had to grow up under the custodianship of many harsh and uncaring relatives. At the age of twelve, he had run away from home and joined the Biafran Army where he saw some of the toughest battles of the civil war. After the war, he had managed to enlist again with the federal army and for twenty-two years he had only been promoted once. He felt deeply victimised but he was always grateful to God because he now had a family of his own no matter how difficult he found it to feed and clothe them. Staying within the folds of the army itself was a bitter struggle. How many times had he slept in the guardroom for the most negligible offenses? How many times had he endured sitting a in cage for weeks underneath the glare of the sun in the barrack exposed to passersby who mocked him and children who laughed at him? How many times had he had his face slapped by junior officers whom he was much older than? Many times, the thought of deserting had crossed his mind but what would he do after he had left the army? He had virtually no marketable skills and had four fast growing children and a young wife to think of. If it had been only him, he wouldn't have thought twice about desertion. The experience of the civil war had trained his body to exist on very little food and on the most unusual things. For instance, eating lizards was no taboo for him. But a man's family is his home and no matter how naturally irresponsible he may be, he had to think about those he brought into this world. He had to struggle to ensure that their lives do not become as hopelessly bitter as his had been. At that was why he remained in the army on a salary that could not be managed for more than one week. He lived on credit and his entire salary was used up within the first week of settling his debts.

He had no savings and no assets of note. All the money he received was used in buying food which never lasted for long. Many days, the children had to go hungry and he would sometimes avoid going home until very late after they had gone to bed. He did so because he could not bear to hear them crying of hunger. Stephanie surprised him one day by sending some food to him. He thought she must have been celebrating something until it became a regular affair. In time, he came to see her as his daily saviour. The only snag about her generosity was that it could not be extended to his children. He felt slightly guilty that he could not carry some of the food to his children who waited for him at the barrack. But at least he forfeited his rations at home to them which made them immensely happy.

The motive behind Stephanie's uncustomary generosity was revealed when she told him that she needed to go out sometimes unaccompanied and that she would henceforth invite a male friend of hers to spend some time with her on an off-and-on basis. Solomon was afraid of what he was getting himself into because his commanding officer had issued strict instructions to the effect that she should not be allowed out alone on any pretext nor should any man be allowed to see her. He knew fully well the consequences of disobeying such strict and explicit orders. Fear did not allow Solomon to say anything let alone object. He needed the daily meals she provided. Stephanie took his silence for compliance. The meals came with greater regularity and in larger qualities but Solomon now ate with more circumspection. He began to have panic attacks that made eating rather unpleasant. Sometimes, he did not even touch the meal and instead wrapped it up and took home to his children. When he wasn't on night duty and was lying with his wife in bed, he would tell her in a manner that seemed enigmatic to her to pray for him. Is there going to be another coup? She would ask and he would reply by shrugging his shoulders. His wife had reason to fearful of coups. Non-

71

commissioned soldiers and indeed soldiers of every rank were wasted at regular intervals on grounds of planning coups, real or imaginary. Corporals would be forced to participate in coups they knew nothing about and ignored afterwards. Life went on whether such coups succeeded or failed. The condition of a poor corporal never seemed to change. Only death and suffering were certain.

One morning when he could no longer bear the torture he went to knock upon Stephanie's door and asked if he could have a word with her. Stephanie, on her part was surprised by his audacity because he was a man who never seemed to talk at all.

Madam ... he began with a stutter , what you are asking me to do is a very big thing ....master would kill me if he knows so I want you to give me a fuck before I die, he stammered without being able to look at her in the eye. Stephanie couldn't believe her ears but she pretended not to have heard him well. Solomon, on his own part, did not have the courage to repeat what he had said. It wasn't that he meant what he had told her and merely wanted to put her in a position as difficult as his but she had not understood. Instead, when she saw that he was incapacitated by indecision, she handed him a monetary note and then dismissed him. Solomon hated himself for his lack of courage but he knew that his family was the main cause of his fear. He did not wish to jeopardise their future with any sort of brazen recklessness.

Shortly afterwards, Stephanie began to go out by herself when the colonel was out of town and she also started to bring in her male friend who turned out to be Oskar Jekker.

Out of desperation and boredom, she had fallen for him. The young intellectual could not believe his luck and followed her all around dumbstruck by the sudden turn of events. As to be expected, Stephanie inspired yet another treatise that became stalled due to inadequate distance from his subject. Oskar threw away discipline and convention and plunged into the pleasures of living flesh. Stephanie taught him how miraculous true passion could be as they wandered from room to room, chasing each other in nakedness. Oskar pondered his ideals of sensuality and the images he saw in his mind delighted him. The entire house rang with laughter any time they were together. They had their baths together and fed each other with an innocence that neither of them had believed they could muster. Although Stephanie was not a stranger to the transports of passion, she was learning again some of its surprises after being blinded to them due to the corrosiveness of materialism. Hitherto, she had chased after money as the sole object of human happiness but when she finally found opulence, she felt empty and bored. In place of contentment, she found a khaki-cladded brute. Opulence without passion makes the heart susceptible to interminable yearning. Only genuine passion could assuage the void that filled her heart and which now threatened to consume her. Oskar provided her an opportunity to give and share. He gave her a reason for laughter that sprang within the depths of her belly. Day by day, Oskar's confidence in himself and in the fondness Stephanie had for him grew until finally he wanted her all to himself. At first, she thought he was joking and teased him. Then she realised he was quite serious. She explained to him that his desires were impractical. What where they to live on? What pot would they piss in? If they eloped, their feelings for one another were certain to vanish because they wouldn't have a hole in which to shit. She pointed out to him that the white bungalow was their only realistic wonderland for now. Oskar had no choice but to accept her logic but with a lot of boyish grumbling. Later, he complained to her that he felt he was being used like a toothbrush to be discarded when it had become worn-out. Stephanie gave him a full kiss and told him to shut up. And so they resumed their games like two little children who only wanted to have fun.

In enjoying the delights of her new lease of life, Stephanie became negligent. She forgot to send Solomon food even though she had been unwittingly jeopardising his life and career. When he was on night duty, Solomon would sit at his post shivering in the cold though he knew Oskar and his master's mistress were enjoying themselves. How forgetful could people become once they found what they wanted? Had Stephanie forgotten so soon? Did she not know the grave consequences of her reckless actions? A few tongues were already wagging in the neighbourhood about her affair and his boss would certainly hear about it in time. He had wanted to warn Stephanie to be more careful but she seemed to have become overwhelmed by her pleasures. What was the point in ruining his own life and hers as well just because a severe bout of reprehensible thoughtlessness had assailed her? Wasn't it better to save himself and the lives of those who depended on him than throw it all away including her life as well? After much agonising, Solomon decided to report her affair to the boss. The opportunity to do so came when he returned from his last trip to the south. Solomon could not tell Umar unequivocally what he had in mind and it was only after his boss had ordered another soldier to give him three slaps did he finally summon enough courage.

There's one man coming to see madam sir.

Since when you fool.

I ---don't ….

You what? Give him three more dirty slaps ! The bloody swine.

The boss' orders were carried out again promptly.

Anytime you travel…

Anytime I travel? So you've been allowing such moral decadence and indiscipline to go on behind my back you bloody fool! After all what I've been doing for you? I will make sure you live to regret this for the rest of your wretched life.

Turning to the soldier who had been doing the slapping he shouted, lock him up in the guardroom for four weeks. By then, I would have thought out what I'll do to him. Solomon was pushed out of the door, cursing within himself his bad luck.

Colonel Umar Zorro did not show himself to Stephanie so that she would still have the impression that he had not returned from his trip. The following night, he loaded an army truck with some soldiers and had them follow him in his own private car to the guest house where his faithless mistress lived. He parked his car outside so as to take her completely unawares and then ordered his men to surround the house quietly in case her lover tried to escape. He pulled out a key from his pocket and opened the front door where he found Stephanie and Oskar lying on the couch in a state of undress watching a movie. They were totally taken by surprise and jumped up together. Umar whipped out a pistol and gave them a wicked grin. He made a few lewd jokes and ordered his troops inside. Stephanie made to put on her clothes but he stopped her with a loud bark. The colonel told his men to bring out all Stephanie's clothes from the wardrobes and tear them to shreds. Zorro's troops carried out the order and soon there were shreds of clothing lying upon the floor. Without any clothes or belongings, Stephanie and her lover were pushed out roughly out of the house. The soldiers taunted them and spat on them. All the while she was weeping uncontrollably, begging for forgiveness from the colonel who remained unmoved. Unable to bear Stephanie's grief, Oskar lurched at their hard-hearted tormentor only to receive a bullet in the gut and then he was carried onto the street to bleed to death. Stephanie's wailing became more hysterical but she too was roughly shoved onto the street. The colonel then barked at them from the gate of the guest house that they had better cleared out of the vicinity or else he would order his men to shoot them like thieves. It was a disturbing spectacle; a young man lying in the middle of the street in a widening puddle of blood was being comforted by a half-naked hysterical woman. A man driving a car stopped and when he saw that Oskar had been shot he wanted to rush off but Stephanie held on to his shirt and begged him desperately to spare their lives. He agreed to carry them to the nearest hospital but the nurses refused to admit them calling them armed robbery suspects. They needed a police report that they had not been involved in an armed robbery operation. Stephanie again fell upon the man to carry them to the next hospital around. Quite reluctantly, he agreed and both of them carried Oskar as carefully as they could back to the car. By then, he was only barely conscious and the back seat of the car was completely covered in blood. The handles of the doors as well the windows were also smeared with blood. Stephanie rushed out of the car and dashed to the reception counter inside the hospital to bring out the nurses. She pleaded with them to accept the handling of the emergency because her own life depended on it. She even threatened to kill herself if they refused to offer Oskar help. The nurses saw that they had no choice so they received Oskar who by then was on the brink of death. The hospital staff started to work in haste to save his life. For more than a week, his condition was critical and nobody knew whether he would survive the ordeal. Within that period, a couple of secret agents came inquiring about his condition as he kept drifting in and out of consciousness in ICU. The secret operatives looked menacing in their dark sunglasses and with large gold chains around their necks. It seemed they wanted Oskar dead at all cost but the skilful hospital officials hindered their efforts. The secret agents went about bribing and threatening newspaper houses not to publish the tragic story or they would be shut down. As to be expected, not a word about the story was published. Oskar lay on the brink of expiration through the bullet of a serving military officer without the nation knowing the truth.

Only Stephanie knew and she stood by him throughout his different states of consciousness and gradually nursed him back to health. When she saw his condition was getting more stable she threatened to tell the world about the colonel's deed. Colonel Umar Zorro turned up with two truck loads of soldiers at her place and threatened her with instant death. The bloodlust looming in his eyes appeared quite real. Stephanie had a change of heart and decided not- to date military men anymore. She wanted nothing more to do with the barbarism of crude khaki boys. The news of Oskar's injury immensely troubled Stephanie's friends and many of them sent him huge and expensive get-well cards, flowers and fruits. He became the major focal point of his hospital floor and Stephanie spent long hours by his side keeping him company and cheering him up. When he was strong enough to be discharged, he moved into Stephanie's room and their relationship became even stronger. She was no longer interested in dating rich middle-aged men and planned to enjoy the remainder of her youth with one of her age. They would both work towards providing their own needs. A few of her old sugar daddies did not mind her new way of life and one or two of them even promised to help her achieve a measure of comfort and stability. She wanted to be a private tutor and they promised to assist her in that direction. Later, she came to realise that she wasn't suited temperamentally to the task and neither did she possess the necessary skills. It then occurred to her to use Olu Ray who had shown some interest in teaching and they could share the proceeds he derived from it. She would find the jobs and he would do them. It sounded good to Oskar.

The next time Olu Ray came around, he was told about the arrangement and he agreed to get involved. Olu Ray could not believe his luck but he concealed it from Stephanie. She had told him that he would be teaching a newly married woman and a girl born into a wealthy family the secrets and delights of the English language. That was just the kind of distraction he sought. For many nights after Stephanie had informed him about what his duties were supposed to be, he would stay awake in his bed watching the webs of spiders on his moonlit ceiling. He would forget about the musty odour in his room that he couldn't dispel. Sheer anxiety kept him awake and he could not think of anything else. Finally, Stephanie took him to Hajia Habiba's abode. It was a brown bungalow located in the coolest residential area in town. Her husband was a top flight civil servant who had just married her the previous year. She couldn't have been more than twenty-two and was extremely beautiful. She was light complexioned and possessed a delicate frame. She appeared to walk with clouds underneath her feet. There was nothing wrong with her English and what she actually wanted to learn was French. But she hoped her tutor would be clever enough to introduce her to stimulating fields of learning. She had had a lot of trouble convincing her husband to allow her acquire some more knowledge. It wasn't conventional to allow one's wife to acquire knowledge under the unusual circumstances she was proposing. To begin with, no man was allowed into the house of another man. It was as clear as that. But Habiba wept incessantly and refused to eat or make love to her husband until he agreed that she may begin to have lessons on the front lawn. Habiba's heart sprang with joy and her excitement increased doubly when she saw the fine young man that was to be her tutor. Stephanie had brought Olu Ray and told him to wait outside the gate while she went in to negotiate the terms of the contract. They were exceedingly generous. Olu would come to the house three times a week to teach her the best of Arabic literature in their English translations and some innocuous European classics. Habiba's husband stressed the fact that he wanted Olu to concentrate almost exclusively on Arabic literature so he spent many days raiding libraries and conducting spasmodic researches into Egyptian, Lebanese, Iranian and Syrian literary arts. His heart and mind came to discover literary treasures he could not find words to describe. He wanted to pour all his ineffable sensations into Habiba's untarnished heart.

On the day he went to give her first lesson, the weather was just about perfect with the dying rays of the sun. The front garden was expertly tended by a couple of old grizzled gardeners. Olu Ray gave his introductory lecture on the symbolism of the veil in not only pan -Arabic literature but nay, in world literature as well. He initiated and sustained discourses on the similarities and differences between western and oriental culture. Later, he came to realise that Habiba wasn't very interested in the grand generalisations of comparative literature but was quite keen on tales of lust, forbidden passion and romantic elopement. And Olu quite happily provided her with such narratives and texts with strict instructions to her to keep them concealed. She would ask, do people really live like that? I mean love like that?

Sure, Olu Ray would reply, what do you think? The best in poetry and fiction can not capture the raptures of the desiring heart. Oh how I wish Habiba that I could only find the right expressions for a tenth of the way great lovers lead their lives. Doesn't your husband show you how beautiful the desires of the heart can be?

Oh don't talk foolish things, such things are only for fictional characters and corrupt people.

Then you are yet to understand the purpose of life if you believe what you say.

Gradually, Olu started to convince Habiba that the tales he read to her were sometimes in fact drawn from real life. He told her that it was selfish for a man to hide from his wife the raptures of unalloyed affection. Humanity made great impressive, if sometimes destructive leaps through the force of passion. Love, the mother of passion gave birth to an unending cycle of myths and mirages. Races that have been unable to see or unwilling to use the energies of passion to ensure their survival have always been doomed to extinction. Olu constructed a devious argument saying that her race had

79

survived up till then because their men did passionate things outside their homes even when they kept their women in purdah. He went on to ask her if it wasn't true that men who kept women in purdah were usually unfaithful to them. And she confirmed that many of such men kept mistresses outside their homes. Habiba's young and inexperienced mind was not able to apprehend the casuistry inherent in Olu's far-fetched revelations. She did not perceive his lack of formulaic rigour. Slowly the germs of rebellion were sown in her heart. She came to despise the clothes tradition demanded her to wear. If only her husband knew the sedition to which she was being exposed. Habiba came to detest the way he desired her. She came to see the hypocrisy behind male-constructed cultures of sexual domination and exploitation. She had been taught to view female enjoyment of sex as indecent and decadent. But Olu taught her that it was all a cultural invention by males who had a morbid fear regarding the powers of female genitalia. It wasn't that his borrowed theories found easy acceptance with her. She could never agree for instance that the penis was a social and cultural construct. That was taking it too far. She needed her cock every now and then up against the lip of her womb and occasionally in the depths of her rectum. She advanced arguments saying that God had created man to rule over women and both the Holy Koran and the Bible corroborate this view. Olu in turn put up rationalistic and atheistic syllogisms indicating the grave cultural bigotry and unsuitability of these world-esteemed texts. He even went as far as propounding the hole-in-the-text theory to Oskar Jekker.

When Olu Ray thought he had sufficiently softened Habiba's heart, he asked her whether she would be interested in allowing him to show her how uplifting egalitarian passion could be. He proposed to guide her through the latest dialectical progressions of human intercourse. At first, she did not quite understand him until he asked if he could see her alone away from the prying eyes of the gardeners and the housemaids.

Habiba became sullen anytime her husband was around. When he asked her what the matter was she complained that she did not see her family enough. And so her husband set aside two days a week for visits to her family. Both Olu Ray and Habiba finally won the chance to be alone. The visits she was to pay her family would provide her the opportunities to see Olu in his room. All his lust-induced agonies were about to end after pinning for months for the merest bit of sensual pleasure. Olu was ready to skip work to be with the most ravishing creature that had ever had the misfortune to reciprocate his feelings. He couldn't think in terms of a long term relationship. It simply wasn't feasible. He was dangling from the face of a steep cliff with his dick. He knew he was toying with death. The community would stone both of them to death if it got a whiff of suspicion. Its ire would be worsened by the fact that he was not a muslim. Habiba would be paraded and humiliated in the streets and then flung to the dogs. No, there was no future for a relationship between them. All they could do was to attempt to fuck with death in the hope they might live to tell the tale. The sex-death nexus is an all-consuming combination. It has a viral power that brings out the edge of existence.

On the day she was to visit him, Olu Ray spent the whole time cleaning and dusting his room. He cooked a fresh pot of stew in case she wanted something to eat and bought an assortment of soft drinks. Every minute of the day his heart ached for her arrival until it became apparent that she wasn't coming. His disappointment was so severe that he could not concentrate for the remaining part of the day. He could not sleep at night either. He decided not to go to work the next day and waited impatiently for the time he would go and give her lessons. When he got there his disappointment was clearly etched on his face. Why he asked, why, and she only replied with a mischievous grin. He made her promise never to cause him so much grief and then fixed another date for the following day.

He missed work the next day as well but he tried as much as possible to control his angst. He could barely cope with the disappointment of the previous day. Seized by a bout of hypocrisy, he found himself praying she should come. He could not wait to hold her dainty body close to his own. His fantasies gave way to troubling vistas of images when he imagined what he would do to her. He paced the edge of the compound where he lived so she would not see him if she should turn up. He was experiencing a meltdown under the delirium of expectation. Then he saw her saunter through the gate. He perceived a tension in her frame as if she had a fear of being seen. Olu did not bother to call her but walked directly behind her so that he could reach her just before she got to the door. It was a good thing that the other tenants were not around to witness her visit. It was certain to have made her incomparably more nervous. He quickly guided her towards his room with his heart thumping wildly.

Her dressing was stunning. She wore a long black satin dress with gold buttons and embroidery. And covering her head down to her waist was an immaculate white shawl. On her feet was a pair of gold sandals to match. In her hands was a parcel neatly wrapped in tin foil.

Why did it take you so long in coming darling?

Don't ask too much questions. Here, she said handing him the parcel. Eat quickly. I haven't got much time to spare.

Olu Ray wasn't very keen on eating just then even though the gift turned out to be huge chunks of roast lamb. They looked really appetising. He put the parcel daintily on a stool and resumed talking to her but she would not listen until he had some of the lamb. Olu had a few bites to please her and then held out the remaining morsel to her. She refused it by shaking her head and insisted that he finish the whole of it.

He complied as he eyed her where she sat on the edge of his bed. He had just noticed that she had taken off her sandals and put on his bathroom slippers which were beside the bed. The nails of her feet had just been painted and the sight of them had a pleasant effect on his senses. To think that she was wearing his own very pair of slippers as she sat looking at him with her lucid child-like eyes. She had made the initial, essential physical contact in such a powerful yet unassuming way. The directness and simplicity of her act was worth a thousand words. Such complete naturalness was certainly the last thing he had expected.

After he had finished eating, Olu Ray moved over to where she sat with the feral grace of a wild creature motivated by a powerful hormonal charge. He put his quivering lips beside her chin and she moved away in a girlish way. His heart was trembling but he knew there was no reason for it. She had come to him. She knew what that meant. They had reached this point by mutual agreement. He removed his slippers from her feet and made her lie gently on the bed. Still, she wouldn't look at him and there was a slight vulnerability about her parted lips. Her head was turned sideways and her eyelids blinked irregularly. Olu Ray wasn't about to pull off the whole of her attire, it would have reduced the enchantment of that rare moment. He wanted to realise his long cherished fantasy of fucking a pseudo-oriental enchantress in full regalia. He also wanted to capture the feel of the biblical Passover when the Israelites had their meals girded and in a hurry with the messenger of death hovering around. It was a real danger to make love to Habiba. It was taboo that she had even come to see him and one of the ways he wanted to stress the fact was by making love to her with her clothes on. He needed to embrace the urgency of their passion. He needed to explore the limits at which such a passion could become dangerous and utterly destructive. He needed to kiss faintly death's broad back as it turned to regard a sea of dark blood and fresh bones.

It wasn't until he had peeled off her gleaming white panties did she look at him directly in the eye. Until they were done she never shifted her eyes from him. For first-timers, they found it pleasing they made slow, unhurried, even-paced love as dark, hidden swords were lurking everywhere within the town.

After it was over, she readjusted her clothes and prepared to go. Olu saw her off to the gate but she prevented him from going any further and hurried off by herself in search of a taxi-cab. Olu Ray stood by till when she had completely vanished from his sight. His Adam's apple went up and down as he swallowed the saliva in his mouth.

Habiba sparked off a chain of thought. What was he doing on this forlorn plain of desert sands? What kind of culture could he possibly aspire to? Oskar had tried to find some purpose in companionship and had received a bullet in the gut for his efforts. Oskar was a beacon of hope to those who aspired to broader cultural horizons. People believed in the audacity of his vision; his yea-saying affirmation was a direct retort to state-sanctioned arsonists who burnt libraries and churches, barbarians who killed dogs and tortured swine, hypocrites who kept women in chains in their houses while they molested beings of twilight zones, bigots who in the name of a single deity proclaimed the deaths of a thousand souls, political opportunists who defiled the nation and pillaged its treasury, primordialists who destroyed the nation's services as they traversed the world looking for gain and pleasure, religionists who despoiled the temples of the land, bastards who fathered clans of homeless offspring, murderers who insisted on keeping the altars clean, slick linguists who turned night into day and vice versa, gluttons who chewed up the country and spat it out into a pit latrine, gun-totting thugs who made war at home and sold the corpses of our dead brothers and sisters to our enemies abroad, con artists who peddled death and shit to us, silver-tongued devils who deprived us the last bit of our heritage, liars who called a rainbow the moon, diseased geezers who shook our hands and then spat into our eyes, mercenaries who fed on their fellow mercenaries, sick arseholes who tore up our arses with their dicks just for the fun of it, shit-eating maniacs who murdered animals just because they resisted, perverted shitheads who slit our throats just because they could, cocksuckers who divided the world between masters and slaves in their sick minds, bumlickers who persisted in devouring their own tails, Satanists who gave the most gorgeous smiles at day time and buried live beings at midnight, ethnocentrists who raided the desert looking for human blood, fuckers who fucked up everything.

*****

Habiba was the experience he was longing for, the dream he had been wanting to fulfil and now that the best had happened. Olu Ray felt a great upsurge of confidence. He did not brag about his luck to anyone but the way in which he carried himself seemed to brand him with some secret success. A new radiance emanated from the hidden recesses of his being. Here, was a land in which he had been warned that forbidden love was impossible and now he had found it at last. Sometimes, he even found it difficult restraining himself from shouting for joy. In this joyous mood, he made friends with Mohammed Isa, one of the tenants who lived behind his building. Mohammed Isa had come to him when he was smiling at the dying sunset because he seemed to be elated. And being filled with so much goodwill, Olu Ray agreed to have a conversation with him.

Mohammed Isa was slender and had small crafty eyes and burnt lips. He spoke with an even tone of voice and seemed to have a curious mind in spite of his average education. Olu Ray learnt that he was married and that his wife had gone on a business trip. Unusual. However, Mohammed Isa explained that since times were hard he allowed her to engage in trading so as to supplement his income. He even seemed broad-minded to Olu when he started to make scandalous revelations about incidents of incest he knew of. Olu could hardly believe his ears but he remained cool and composed. Soon Mohammed Isa was inviting him into his DON'T ENTER abode to have games of scrabble and monopoly but he wasn't interested and made acceptable excuses to let himself off the hook. It wasn't that Olu felt snobbish about becoming too intimate with him. On the contrary, he was glad having struck up an acquaintance with a fundamentalist of a markedly different species. This was a man who had a boldly printed sign in front of his quarters saying DON'T ENTER holding out his hand in civilised friendship. True, Isa's beliefs and attitudes towards Olu were sharply opposed contradictions but the latter saw no point in paying extra-ordinary attention to them. He took it to be one of those odd things.

Then some days later, he saw a smallish woman dressed in Arabic fashion enter into the compound carrying two heavy looking carrier bags walking towards Mohammed Isa's quarters. Moments later, she came out again this time carrying an empty bucket which she took to the pump meant for the entire compound. Olu who wasn't too far from where she was greeted her and asked whether she was Isa'a wife and she answered in the positive. He then asked her about her journey and a few casual questions until he was interrupted by Mohammed Isa's arrival. When Olu looked into his face, he saw a hard look on it and Isa didn't reply his wife when she greeted him even though they hadn't seen each other for a while.

At night, Olu heard a heavy fall of blows coming from Isa's quarters accompanied by the distant cries of a woman. When the wailing increased to an intolerable point, Olu ventured out of his room to see what was going on and he saw Isa's wife still wailing carrying a travelling bag. When he asked her what the matter was, she told him that her husband had been beating her just because he had seen her exchange a few words with him. Olu could not believe his ears but he quickly returned to his room to avoid a prolongation of Isa's wrath. Mohammed Isa had also appeared from behind. He started to swear at her again and she too swore back at him and then he rained more blows on her until he had driven her out of the compound. The other tenants peeked out of their doorways for a few moments to see what was going on and disappeared again not wanting to get involved.

The following day, Isa's wife was brought back by her mother because as the saying goes a wife stays in her husband's home. She had to remain with her man in thunder, lighting and rain. She had to remain chained to his bed and fireless hearth. She had to remain shackled to his time, his pain and his pleasure. She had to remain and not run away. From then on, Olu Ray never saw her again and he did not venture to look the way of Mohammed Isa's quarters. There was after all no cause for him to do so since he had Habiba. And furthermore, he soon got himself a new catch.

Aisha was seventeen and unmarried and her father was quite wealthy. Her father was uncouth and he passed this drawback on to his extensive brood. In the morning, the first thing he reached for was his chewing stick which he gnawed with violent jaws. He hardly ever had a bath and went about doing his business in soiled dirty clothes. Furthermore, he couldn't write his own name and only had a rough idea of how much he was worth. Minions pilfered large sums of money from him because of his ignorance. What he planned was that Aisha would learn some English for a few months and then he would marry her off to one of his rich old friends. But Aisha had other plans in mind for herself. As to be expected, the scope for improvement was circumscribed by the unavailability of the right sort of exposure. The necessary cultural background was simply lacking. Her uncouth father hardly ever spoke to her unless he wanted to reprimand her. When he had cause to admonish her, it was usually in a rough manner. In their compound, all her father's children from different wives shouted all day long in torn dirty clothes, cursing and fighting each other. One found it difficult to even read even a few pages from a simple story book or a newspaper. The noise levels were simply unbearable.

Aisha was like queen to her siblings because of her kind-heartedness. They came to her with their grievances and quarrels and she would attend to them with a patience that was beyond her years. When Olu Ray started to teach her English, he had no intention of having an affair with her because it just didn't occur to him that she might have the appropriate emotional apparatus. Her basic good nature did not automatically guarantee the passionate involvement Olu Ray craved. Between lessons, she would divulge to Olu pieces of information that could be regarded as minor oriental slabs of wisdom with a pure-toned voice. They developed an immediate friendliness towards each other; an off-hand way of relating to one another which Olu thought could not be transformed into something corporeal. Then he started to study her face more closely. It was spotless and had an average complexion that could become ravishing with the aid of appropriate cosmetic devices. Judging from the size of the bulge underneath her scarf, Olu could tell that she didn't have very long hair. But her most endearing asset was the warmth of her smile. And although it seemed guileless there was an almost discernable influence in its warmth. Her physical features appeared to change from day to day. Sometimes she seemed soft and feminine. On other days, she had a large-boned country girl quality that robbed her of subtlety, grace and delicate sensuality. A lot of her discussions with Olu were surprisingly deep and it was her words that made him to explore the nature and breadth of her mind more closely. Her mind appeared to call out of the depths and her body followed many leagues behind. Nothing she uttered gave her away as being the kind of girl to be toyed with outside of wedlock. Without a hint of pique, she would denounce the widespread occurrence of teenage pregnancies and the corrupting influence of lecherous old men who could not keep their baggy cotton pants up. At times, Olu would be so impressed by her foresight and values and assured himself that he had at least found someone who had been saved. This warm feeling prompted him to invite her to his place. At home she had developed a formidable reputation as a model of respectability and chastity and no one really bothered with her movements. She also did well to cultivate a measure of genuine discreetness. So the few times her absence was noticed, it was believed that she had gone after a good cause.

The first time Olu invited her over was an occasion he committed to memory. As usual, he had left work to go to the market to get some foodstuffs accompanied by a driver who worked with the bank. He was called Frizi. Frizi had four kids and a young wife but life was made difficult by abysmal poverty. Because Frizi could speak the dialect, Olu sometimes invited him to come shopping with him. As compensation, Olu would buy him some groundnuts and sugar-cane which provided him with lunch. All through his life, Frizi had had an extremely rough time. He had had to run away as an orphaned boy from the house of a mean and selfish uncle. At a bus terminal, he had indicated he wanted to be taken anywhere north and he got what he really desired; stranded by the desert. He could not find work for months after his arrival and had to sleep at open bus stations amid much grease and grime. At mornings, he would walk to a stream three kilometres away to have a bath. Thieves and hoodlums did not bother with him because he had deposited the few things he had at the police station. Also, from his bare and filthy appearance there wasn't much to steal. His looks were no different from any other ruthless armed robber. When he found luck in securing a job, Frizi was fortunate enough to marry a local uneducated girl.

Soon after the marriage, kids started coming. As a bachelor, Frizi never had any enduring worries. He had lived only for the moment but the arrival of his children had now granted him a sense of responsibility he never knew he possessed. The bank was like a blood-sucking monster with a multinational reach, outlook and methods; one slaved until one became stupid and useless from the onslaught of routine and vertigo, until one finally suffered the loss of good health, until one faced death with a pathetic and broken-down body. It was then that the company discarded one like mere used paper. The painful part of the matter was that the long years spent in service went so quietly by without the kind of vibrancy more active persons sought. One flitted through life like a nameless shadow. Everyday, people like Frizi just managed to get through with little or nothing to eat. Languishing in squalor with a bunch of starving children had become his accepted lot in life. Yet, the fight for daily survival could not be abandoned even as the pitiless struggle grew to be almost pointless. Penury gnarled everything; withered faces, twisted veins in the neck, discoloured broken teeth, sick malformed limbs, incessant vendetta over the loss of a couple of coins, bitter wives, dispossessed children, leaking roofs, broken toilets, dry wells, ant-eaten sticks of furniture, shabby clothes, shoes with holes, smelly living quarters, saltless soups, incest caused by over-crowding and so on. It didn't make sense to talk about decent living standards when all notions of decency had become lost. Being able to maintain the right to air was decent enough. One would certainly be asking for too much if one had more than a meal a day and it didn't have to be decent. That would be asking for too much.

At the market gates where to be found groups of mendicants as usual. Many of them were blind and had to be piloted around by young relatives while they cried loudly for alms. Others had been incapacitated by acute leprosy and other diseases and untreated sores. There were crippled mothers who crawled about in the dust with their children trailing them behind. Many of the children were wailing with snot running down the faces in the intense heat. Flies buzzed over the heads of the beggars sometimes entering their mouths and noses. Hammers rose and fell at a construction site nearby making an unpalatable din. Spittle issued forth from toothless mouths and dried up in the dust.

Olu wanted to buy some groundnut oil so he went towards a line of seated old women who sold edible oil with Frizi beside him. Olu was quite finicky when buying the bottle of oil because there were so many types of adulterated oil in the market. Some even had been blended with crude oil. When heated such types of oil turned into black sediment on the frying pan. Once in the stomach it felt like rock. It took days to be expelled from the system. They got the remaining items he needed and they made their way outside the market; out of the boisterous arcade of commerce, the stench of meat and blood, the endless buzzing of flies, puddles of brackish water, palm oil-stained narrow passageways, rude traders, duplicitous sellers, lopsided kiosks, muddy thoroughfares, unbalanced benches and tables, wailing babies, soiled nappies, misery, poverty, disease and greed.

When Olu got home, he prepared some food in anticipation of Aisha's visit. And she did come. She would not have anything to eat and she had a sweet artless smile all the time on her face. Olu talked to her about a number of casual things until he could no longer contain his desire to make love to her. He made an awkward dash at her and began to pull off her clothes and surprisingly she made only the flimsiest attempts at resistance. In the culture, such kinds of romantic resistance were the norm. Some girls went to the extent of scarring men's bodies with bites. Making love seemed like a tussle between wild cats or large serpents.

Olu soon had a fine young girl all naked before him. He just couldn't believe his luck as he scrambled out of his clothes. Then an unforeseen agony confronted him. Though she was naked she wouldn't allow him to make love to her. He started to say idiotic things to allay her fears and to assure her that he cared for her. Aisha didn't say anything but it was obvious her discomfort had not been dispelled. Olu kissed her face, eyes, neck, shoulders in order to make her feel more comfortable. He tried to gave her a full kiss on the mouth but she pulled away.

After all, hadn't she been kept behind closed doors all her life and indoctrinated to view sex with infidels as dirty and immoral? Hadn't she been trained all along to suppress her sensuality and sexuality by both well-respected men and women in her community? Olu had a faint idea of the constraints of her background and his desire to trample over it grew. He only wanted to fuck. Why did it have to be such a big deal? But she could not understand him. She saw him instead as a predator, a male tyrant that any right-thinking girl should resist underneath a shroud of passivity and subjection. God had put between her legs a very precious and expendable fruit that must be protected at all cost. That was what was always being drummed into her. There was no doubt that she had strong feelings for Olu but she just couldn't give in like that. She had to persist in proclaiming her innocence and chastity. Her scythe must be held high above her head as barbarians stormed the gates leading to her anteroom. Olu would find her gates hard to break. Sweat poured out of Olu's struggling body while she continued to evade him without a drop of sweat from hers. They struggled up and down the length and breadth of the bed but Aisha continued to resist with an inexplicable mix of defiance and grace. A few times, Olu even gave up the struggle but he continued to be lured by her poise, by the civility of her resistance. There must have been a curious game she was playing. To begin with, she agreed for him to undress her and now she wouldn't agree to fuck. Was this some meaningful erotic ploy lodged in the annals of tradition? Was he expected to say or do something for everything to fall into place? Olu could not fully crack the mystery but he resolved to persist until some sort of answer revealed itself to him. He resumed his carnal struggle with yet more vigour and more trickles of sweat broke out of his body. Once more, she took him through the length and breadth of the rumpled bed with moves orchestrated by tactics and strategy. There was a Napoleonic skill with which she conducted her retreats. When Olu finally hit the cunningly guarded fortress, his efforts gave him very little pleasure, it had been a pyrrhic victory.

She wasted no time in putting on her clothes without still a bead of sweat on her while Olu Ray looked as if he had been doused with a bucket of scalding water. After their first uncomfortable encounter at lovemaking, things were comparatively easier afterwards. After all, she hadn't been a virgin but she had behaved as if she had been one. But who needed virgins anyway, Olu thought to himself. All he could think was fuck all that. On a corporeal level, Olu started to communicate with her using the blunt wordless language of direct, unalloyed sex. It wasn't that she offered herself to him as an over-ripe water melon to be used and abused as he saw fit. But at least she never tried to get him to break his neck in a struggle to have sex with her. Olu even tried teaching her how to kiss but he found he hadn't the patience. Once, after realising he always thought of having sex when she was with him she said to him; why is your penis always standing up when I'm sitting by you? Olu wanted to congratulate her on her insight but he also felt ashamed of his behaviour. He had been an outright swine and there was no question about that the validity of her comment. The word penis lingered in his troubled conscience. It had sounded unbearably archaic the way she employed it. It certainly would have been much better if she had used prick, cock or dick which though vulgar, were far more tolerable at a moment that had the feel of a post-coital comedown. Olu nonetheless had clearly underestimated the level of Aisha's sensitivity, insight and power of expression

Olu's relationship with Habiba and Aisha had done much in lifting his self-esteem.

Even his co-tenants started to view him with a combination of admiration and envy. He was no longer a shadow that drifted back and forth out of the yard. His sex life was simply a dream. There was another tenant who was even more madly in love. Her name was Linda Bello and she was a Christian northerner. She wasn't very pretty but had a terrific figure and she also had a polish Olu admired. There was a tall quiet medical doctor who was in love with her and who kept coming to see her at all hours. Linda was about thirty-two years old and her man must have been at least four years older yet they were behaving like a couple of love-crazed kids. It was slightly preposterous. The doctor would come and spend about three nights at her place and then Linda would repay the visit by spending almost a week at his crib. They didn't seem to have any independent existence and led more or less symbiotic lives. Linda was a fast walker and she always appeared to be hurrying to preserve her love, her horde and whatever. Yet, any experienced person could tell that their passion would burn out eventually but what was difficult to divine was how and when. The two love birds kept hurrying about to build a nest for their love. Then one night Olu heard Linda crying-love had surely flown away because it didn't have a sufficiently strong nest in which to settle. He wanted to go into her room to console her but he stopped himself because there was a way in which aggrieved souls took advantage of their sympathisers. For two whole days, Linda would not come out of her room and when she finally did, she had started to come to terms with her loss. Yet, Olu was careful about lavishing condolences upon her. He did not want to become her weeping bag. Olu had always known that Linda was attracted to him but there had been nothing he could do with the doctor around. He had also made up his mind not to become a second fiddle for her affections. One night, Linda held Olu's hand and led him through the darkness to her room. He went with her without saying a word. He thought she was taking him to pour out her love sorrows on him for yet another time. The lights in her room were on and Olu could see that she only had a shawl about her. She pulled him down to her bed and started to moan beneath him. She had nothing on. She pulled him closer still and continued to moan. She smelt fresh and organic at the time. It was a seductive fragrance. Olu sidled to her breasts and started to kiss them and then he moved down again to her navel which he also kissed. Suddenly, he stood up and walked to the door; where are you going? she asked and he said to her, get over your last affair before you start another one. The bitterness oozing out of you is too thick for me. He crossed the threshold of her room and she shouted fuck you at his diminishing back. Olu could forgive himself for rejecting her offer for sex because he had Habiba and Aisha. There was no point in complicating his sex life with a third dimension and an exhausted one for that matter.

Life continued as usual for Olu. Soon after, Habiba paid him yet another visit. Only that this time she was a little moody. Their love-making was a little different. Olu had been trying to expose Habiba to the exotic concept of female liberation. In his most liberal moments, he would call himself a feminist and vow to become a househusband in the future. Once in this mood, he encouraged Habiba to express her sexual preferences and fantasies and soon enough he broke through her inhibitions and as to be expected the results were wild. Habiba came to play a very prominent role in bed. Olu admired her courage even though it exhausted him. She could not believe what she had been missing and came to despise her hypocritical husband's way of hiding the light from her. On subsequent occasions when her husband had sex with her, she remained like a log of wood and wore a deep frown. The way he did it was so uninspiring. Many times, she felt like showing him how to do it right but a slight fear held her back. She knew he would be greatly offended and that he would be forced to inquire into the matter thoroughly until her secrets emerged. The two men in her life confused her greatly. At a level, she could not accept the drive for female liberation because she believed Allah created women subservient. She even believed that women who upheld the unIslamic doctrine were doing the devil's work and she was ready to take up the sword against them. But she felt better about the demand for better sex amongst women. Men like her husband ought to be far considerate in the bedroom. It was the considerateness she discovered in Olu that made her want to keep him as her lover. She used to tell him or rather beg him to preserve his body for her. Her hope was dashed when one day she discovered Aisha in his room. She simply told him he was finished and walked out of his door. Olu knew he was truly finished because when she got home she complained to her husband that he had been making passes at her. It was now a matter of how long he could keep at bay the danger that was now inexorably dragging towards him.

Aisha on the other hand continued to visit him but she became more exacting in her demands. She had grown to realise that there was more to love than sex. Just because she couldn't speak English properly doesn't mean she wasn't entitled to some respect. She started to fight almost tooth and nail for her idea of respect. First of all, she began to resist his demands for sex and then she started to ask to be taken out. And Olu, on his part, started to respect her more. He knew she had to make strenuous efforts to expand her mind. It wasn't a task that could be accomplished in a few weeks or even months and it wasn't also clear whether she could make the kind of effort required. If she wasn't able to achieve this near impossible task, Olu was ready to let her seek her respect elsewhere. She herself had started to allude to this possibility but he knew it wasn't as easy as that. And all over again, Olu had began to experience the pains and drawbacks of romantic entanglement.

What Olu had wanted initially was pure uncomplicated sex. He wanted to call his lover for a late afternoon chat and discuss the main events of the day and then have a nice simple fuck afterwards. But it was not so simple. His desires belonged to the realm of fantasy and animality. Only animals could copulate with minimal consequences. On the human scale, there were the vagaries of love to contend with, carved stones of civilisation to be burnished and maintained, regulations of society to be observed. All of these entail complex and elaborate rules and so he could not have simple uncomplicated sex like a beast. He was only able to conceive of such fantasies in the pornographic stretch of his imagination. Society would never allow him to fuck like an animal.

*****

Surprisingly, Hugo wasn't as fortunate as a libertine in building a library of memory consisting a catalogue of erotic images; paintings of naked nymphs and boy kings, movies of transgression and debasement, fragments from decadent literature and importantly, the erupting bodies of nubile girls imprisoned by religion and ancient philosophies of the cock. It wasn't that he had no chances open to him, quite on the contrary. A certain Alhaji Sule Mukhtari had fallen in love with him and this happened in such an ordinary manner. Being a wit, people usually found Hugo quite likeable. They had met in the house of a mutual friend where Hugo had put on effeminate airs for a joke and there and then he caught Mukhtari's eye. He began insisting that Hugo should follow him to his place. It was an attractive pad, complete with stereo set, colour TV, and DVD player. In short it was a bachelor's dream hang-out. There was also a large refrigerator stocked with food and drinks and Mukhtari made Hugo welcome any time. Hugo was taken aback by his new friend's hospitality and warmth but he did not read any meanings into them.

The relationship started becoming a bit unbearable for Hugo when Mukhtari started to insist that he came to see him all the time. He could not understand the sudden and strange attraction Sule Mukhtari had for him so he watched the turn of events. An appointment was made that Hugo would teach Mukhtari to cook but the former could not make the date because he was held up by his work. Mukhtari was so disappointed that he sulked for a few days. When he felt better, he even suggested that Hugo should leave his job so he could find another one for him but he politely declined the offer. In the midst of company, Mukhtari would laugh hysterically at any witty thing Hugo uttered but he didn't laugh much when they were alone together. He always seemed to be in earnest gazing into Hugo's elusive eyes. Sometimes, if Hugo was lying on the bed, Mukhtari would join him and begin to caress his back while Hugo continued to crack jokes. He was always fighting off his worst fears. Mukhtari also had an intense passion for pornographic movies which he showed endlessly when his friend was around. Hugo too viewed them keenly but with a pure heterosexual interest. After they had finished watching porn, Hugo would go into the kitchen to cook for two because Mukhtari couldn't bear to eat alone when his friend was around. And they had to eat from the same dish. Mukhtari would sometimes put a morsel of fish or a piece of meat into the mouth of the hard-playing object of his desire. When Hugo thought more deeply about Mukhtari's strange behaviour, he decided that he was only interested in spoiling him like a kid brother. He wished Mukhtari would give him some money from time to time because he could always do with a little more money.

But he never did and Hugo never had enough courage to ask. It hadn't occurred to him yet that Mukhtari was treating him like a lowlife geisha demanding to know his movements and wanting a say as to what his behaviour should be. When he told Hugo that he had a fiancée and was about to get married to her, the latter was genuinely happy for him. He never took Hugo to visit her though. Instead, he took him to see her hospitalised father who was recovering from a stroke. The old man had a small frame and a tonsured head. He had beady and cunning eyes as well. He spoke slowly with a deep and grovelly voice begging Allah to spare his life until after the wedding. He told Mukhtari that he could do whatever he wished with his daughter once he had been married. Mukhtari, on his part, nodded politely to anything the old man said. When they got out of the hospital, Hugo asked if he could come to the imminent wedding but Mukhtari said he couldn't. Mukhtari refused Hugo's request perhaps because mistresses and male lovers were never allowed to come near the home. Hugo feigned slight disappointment and Mukhtari bought him some roast meat to appease him. Hugo ate gladly and sang for Mukhtari as they went along. This pleased Mukhtari immensely.

When they got back to his house, he slotted in a porn movie as usual and came to sit by Hugo's feet as he sometimes did gazing to his eyes. Then he held his hands and started to stroke them gently. They were warm and sweaty. Mukhtari removed his red skull cap and placed it on the centre table to reveal his balding head. Hugo pretended to be engrossed with the film and pulled himself to a straighter position when he was clutched by his waist. There, he remained looking into the seemingly uninterested eyes of Hugo. They were glued upon the television screen. Mukhtari moved further up still and tried to kiss Hugo who turned his head sharply away to avoid the bristles of his chin.

Mukhtari tried again and brushed Hugo's smooth cheek with his lips. It was then Hugo told him to desist because such acts made him fantasise wildly about girls. Mukhari got angry or perhaps pretended to be and demanded that he should spend the night with him. Hugo made an excuse of not informing the people he lived with that would be spending the night away. Mukhtari was only partially placated and complained that it had never occurred to Hugo to spend the night with him and he wasn't being a loyal friend. Mukhtari claimed he did everything to ensure that he was happy and all he got for his efforts was nothing but ingratitude. He then selected another date for Hugo to spend the night with him which was fixed for the following day. On the following day, Hugo did not appear as planned and this broke Mukhtari's heart. Mukhtari went to where he stayed on three separate occasions that night but Hugo was no where to be found. He drove about town with his full lights on and his heart burning with longing and hope that he would find his evasive tormentor. He found no luck so he drove back home to lie on his cold empty bed.

Hugo knew Mukhtari would be pinning away and didn't want him to suffer too much so he decided to pay him a visit. True enough, Mukhtari was sulking. Hugo made him a present of a stack of porn magazines to appease but he was only half successful. Mukhtari then suggested they pass the night at Hugo's. Hugo did not make a commitment. Mukhtari set a date to come over on new year's eve to help Hugo fight away loneliness as he called it.

On the last Friday before new year's eve, Mukhtari went as usual to attend the jumat service at the mosque. There, all twelve of Stephanie's former boyfriends and Habiba's husband were gathered. After the service, some of them re-congregated outside the mosque to discuss the corrupting decadence of invading Christians. Habiba's husband told them the story of how his wife was nearly seduced by an infidel. There and then it was decided that Olu Ray would be killed. The men debated recommended ways of dying for Olu. They could stone him to death in broad daylight. They could chop off his arms and let him bleed to death. They could have him beheaded and then mount his head on spike which would be paraded in all the neighbourhoods of town as a deterrent to others. They could have him castrated and hurled into the district of eunuchs. There were so many forms of punishment they could inflict on the infidel. But one thing was certain, there would be no forgiveness for the lecherous swine. He was a filthy pig and would be treated as such. He would be poked and prodded until his pelt became a blood-soaked carpet. He would be taken to the stretch of desert where vultures did their work on the flesh of the dead.

The Prophet Mohammed (peace be upon his name) would have frowned upon such sacrilege and all those who condoned it. Then someone complained about the activities of invited Christian preachers who were said to be up to no good. There was unanimous disapproval of this disturbing development and all swore by the name of Allah to stamp it out with the hooves of the horses of jihad. What was needed by a tiny spark, an excuse to set ablaze the torches of purification. The twelve jilted alhajis complained about the alarming spread of venereal diseases all because of the influx of infidels. Some of them were honest enough in admitting to knowing the scourge first-hand but had now returned to the path of righteousness. Two men were particularly put off by the single-testicled alhaji because they believed he was incurably decadent so they plotted to kill him. Others were informed about the plan and most agreed with it since it was for the cause of the faith. Alhaji Hankali, the hapless man was to be killed with a knife and deposited in front of the Catholic Church to make it appear like the Christians had done it. Fair enough all agreed again. Two days later, the plan was carried out, Alhaji Hankal's naked body was dropped in front of the only Catholic Church within the mainly Islamic town. Fear coursed through the entire rank and file of the local Christian community. A world renowned Christian evangelist from the United States was scheduled to speak in a few days time and some of the church leaders were strongly contemplating calling it off. There were clear indications that there was going to be a bloodbath. Many Christians started to leave the agitated town in droves carrying along the properties they had spent their lifetimes amassing. Dozens of trucks and trailers carrying Christians left at dawn and at dusk.

Their muslim friends with whom they had ate and played together started to hiss at them calling them scoundrels and filthy dogs. The sudden change was hard to believe. But not all Christians left the tense town as the authorities kept assuring them that the peace of the ancient town would not be disturbed. But their assurances were in vain because the following morning before the sun had come up, thousands of sword-carrying defenders of Islam went about chanting holy songs of war. They headed towards the Catholic Church-built during the colonial era- and set the whole edifice ablaze. Then they went to another church and found some Christians in prayer inside. The women were raped and then brutally killed with swords. The men within were swiftly put to the sword as well. Fifty-six persons lost their lives in that church alone. A total of forty churches were razed by Islamic incendiaries. Brothels were sacked and prostitutes were also brutally raped and murdered. The residential homes of Christians were not spared and many of such homes were razed to the ground. For an entire week, mob law prevailed in the town, the lynchings and burning went on unabated until those holding high positions in government decided that the international community could get to know about what was going on and decided to put a stop to it. Anti- riot squads were mobilised to shoot anyone on sight and well over a thousand souls lost their lives in the process. Many of them were Muslims because they were the ones intent of wiping out the degeneracy of Christians . The anti-riot squads were particularly ruthless in their killings and many of them even joined the rampaging Muslims in looting Christian shops. Property valued in millions was lost in the looting. The streets were filled in no time with stinking dead bodies which were later ordered to be burnt to check the spread of cholera, typhoid and other epidemic diseases that had already reared their heads in the town.

In the official bulletin released by the government, it was stated that only one hundred and sixteen persons lost their lives but the independent press knew better yet it could not publish more realistic figures because it feared to offend the government. The lands on which the burnt churches stood were confiscated by government so as not to provoke further hostilities. Local journalists were harassed and threatened with death if they published true accounts of what happened. No inciting releases were allowed – in fact the authorities encouraged a total black out on the affair. Not a word was to be mentioned. And as usual, the most powerful journalists were bribed to keep to their own end of the deal. A photo journalist who dared to release a photograph displaying Muslims in an orgy of burning was killed by a letter bomb. Later, he was made a martyr but the memory of the more than one thousand souls who lost their lives in the riots was immediately forgotten. The emir assured everyone that the lives of the remaining Christians would be protected but many viewed them as empty words. They took to the roads in spite of anti-riot men who had been stationed at strategic points to discourage them. Some even openly restricted their leaving; so much for freedom of movement. Those who remained in town did so largely because they feared to provoke the wrath of anti-riot squads. The Christians now had no churches in which to worship and stayed within the confines of their homes calling the name of sweet Jesus. The emir did not want the Christians to leave the town because they provided a sizeable proportion of the skilled manpower and moreover local commerce depended almost completely on their involvement. Perhaps what was needed was planned periodic massacres of Christians so they wouldn't become too pervasive and hence strong. They could be decimated under the guise of religion. Religion was a powerful rallying point. It never failed to provoke the irrepressible ire of street kids who found opportunities to be busy. This was a moot idea though. During the riots, Hugo had taken refuge in Olu Ray's room to hide from the relentless desires of Alhaji Mukhtari. The two friends remained indoors throughout the rioting, burning and looting thinking about the future of their land and people, thinking about their own young lives. The plundering and mass destruction went on all in the name of Allah who seemed from all empirical indications to have coolly detached himself from man's reality and hence the scenes of the carnage. He may have completely deconstructed himself to make way for more intriguing possibilities and had perhaps established new theological exigencies and conditions yet unknown to humankind. Indeed a sad period of probabilities. Hugo wished humankind would in turn rise to meet the challenges of the degenerate period for a healthier employment of its energies. He hoped that the seed of this idea would find the appropriate soil and germinate into full power. But as always ideas take time in getting around and invariably every realised idea becomes in the long run, an anachronism if it succeeds in not becoming an abortion. The short time Olu Ray and Hugo spent together was probably the happiest they had as friends. Hugo narrated to his friend how his conscience had been troubled by the advances of Mukhtari. Perhaps he would have considered yielding to Mukhtari's pressures if he had been more handsome and younger. Olu Ray then took him up and started to call him wife as a tease. Hugo took his jokes in good faith and even replied he was ready to sleep with any man once he had enough money to spend. He was disappointed by Stephanie Machi, the *femme fatale*, for falling in love with an impecunious jerk like Oskar Jekker. He felt it was a result of a sudden disease in her mind. They had meals which they took so much care in preparing together, the killings notwithstanding. One night, when they had gone to sleep on Olu Ray's large single bed, something slightly unusual happened. Olu Ray who had his back turned towards Hugo felt his waist suddenly jerking towards his back side. It was only when Hugo's hand had clasped him did he shove him off. For a couple of hours, he remained awake pondering the incident. He couldn't talk it over with his friend who appeared to be still asleep and wished he was knowledgeable in the interpretation of dreams and the science of the unconscious and semi-conscious. There were a few issues he needed to understand for the peaceful repose of his animus. He had no urge to blame anyone, least of all, Hugo. He needed just a little more understanding, that's all. The following morning neither of them referred to the incident and they went about their business as cheerfully as before. Olu Ray had become tired of staying indoors and so he asked Linda to take him with her to see some of her friends. She had since mellowed so she agreed. Hugo wasn't interested in going so he remained indoors to sleep some more. Whilst Olu Ray was away, something tragic happened. Habiba's husband taking advantage of the internecine upheaval sweeping through the town sent some vicious thugs to murder Olu in his room. On getting there, the thugs didn't even bother to check out who was sleeping on the bed before they brought down their rough-hewn clubs upon his head. Hugo died in his sleep with his blood splattered upon the sheets and wall. It wasn't the handiwork of clinical serial killers, it was like the rage of lunatic butchers.

When Olu Ray came back to see the dastardly act, he went absolutely berserk screaming his head off continuously for more than thirty minutes. Only a few people were still sensate enough to feel the pangs of pain caused by Hugo's death. A melancholic amnesia seemed to be flowing everywhere. Death had stalked the town too brazenly and incisively to arouse any feelings of horror or disgust. Almost everyone had lost a loved one and had a lot of crying and grieving to do.

A few noble servants headed by Olu Ray did not want Hugo's memory to vanish as instantly as death had taken him so they got the government to acknowledge his death. It took several letters, several battles and even blood coupled with sweat to accomplish. Eventually, the government allowed the noble servants to honour their dead member in whatever way they thought benefiting. After all, he had died in service. The graveyard where Hugo was buried had a melancholy cast, so many thickly leaved trees above old unkempt graves. A group of friends held a small wake-keeping ceremony for Hugo. They couldn't have anything elaborate for Hugo at the edge of the desert. No one had the physical strength and presence of mind. Everyone was trying to conserve their energies for the long harsh journey out of the desert into lush savannah country.

The utter dereliction of the area Hugo's grave was located provided an unmistakable contrast to the energy and imagination with which he had conducted his life. He might have wished that all his friends came to party wildly right on top of his grave with bowls of punch, fine pot and a bunch of crazy girls. Hugo would perhaps be smiling in his grave giving the finger to the shrine and the well-constructed altar, the faceless hack further obscured by a million masks toiling away in a nondescript building, the artificial boundaries and categories of community and numerous other constraints that create grotesque parodies of free-living and free-loving beings.